Cernunnos Books
The Bowl Full of Blood

Devakinandan Khatri (1861-1913) was a pioneer of Hindi fiction. He is remembered for his fantasy thrillers *Chandrakanta, Chandrakanta Santati* and *Bhootnath,* but his role in shaping an important part of modern Indian culture is not well known. He used Hindi in the *nagari* script, and his works were so popular in the 1890s that people learned the script just to be able to follow them. Later, Mahatma Gandhi adopted Hindi as a vehicle for his independence struggle. Devakinadan Khatri founded a literary magazine, *Upanyaas Lahari,* and ran a publishing house, *Lahari Press.* Interestingly, his son, Durgaprasad Khatri completed Bhootnath after his death in the form of *Rohtaas Math,* and his great-grandson Vivek Khatri has written a sequel to *Rohtaas Math.*

Balwant Kaur, born in Delhi, has taught Hindi at Miranda House, Delhi University, since 2001. She has an M.A. and a Ph.D. in Hindi. She has had several essays, studies and translations published in journals. She is associated in an editorial role with the prestigious Hindi literary magazine *Hans,* founded by Premchand and revived by Rajendra Yadav. She has edited *Rajendra Yadav Rachnaavali* ("The Complete Works of Rajendra Yadav"), and five other books and special issues.

A.K. Kulshreshth is the author of *Once Upon a Time in the Future,* a short story collection based on the Hindu epic *Mahabharat.* His short stories have appeared in literary magazines and anthologies in seven countries.

Devakinandan Khatri

# THE BOWL FULL OF BLOOD

With an afterword by
Balwant Kaur

And 12 illustrations by
Zoya Chaudhary

Translated from Hindi by
A.K. Kulshreshth

Cernunnos
BOOKS

Originally published in Hindi as *Virendraveer athva katora bhar khoon*
in Varanasi, India, in 1895

This translation © Cernunnos Books Pte. Ltd., 2015
http://www.cernunnosbooks.com/

Cover illustration and design by Zoya Chaudhary
Illustrations © Zoya Chaudhary
Hindi advisors: Archana Verma, Balwant Kaur
English literary advisors: Desirée Ward, N. Henaff
Interior design: N. Henaff

ISBN: 981-0950-52-7
ISBN-13: 978-981-0950-52-1

## Chapter One

“PEOPLE SAY that good begets good, and evil begets evil. Today, I will inflict evil on a good woman and faithful wife. If I do a good job of it, I will become Prime minister tomorrow. Who will say, then, that the evil do not enjoy happiness, or that the good do not suffer misfortune? All I have to do is to be firm. I must not let her beauty and her sweet words melt my heart… Who's that? Someone comes this way!”

It was past midnight, and dark clouds had laid an inky shroud upon the earth. In the deathly quiet, the only sound was that of the rustling leaves as gusts of wind shook them. A man hidden inside a cluster of grape vines mumbled the above words to himself. What did he look like? It is difficult to say right now,

*"No! I won't let you go!" the woman said.*

dear reader. Firstly, the dark night hid him well. Secondly, he was swathed in black clothes. Thirdly, the leaves of the grape vines formed a curtain that hid his features. He will reveal himself later in this story, dear reader, but for now, he was biding his time. He gnashed his teeth as he gazed at a small bungalow in the centre of the garden.

The bungalow was adorned by pretty creepers. In one of its rooms, the light from a candle showed a couple talking and gesturing. The tiny bungalow had an octagonal layout, with eight chair-like platforms along each side. Its roof was a mesh of bamboo covered with dense foliage. A wax candle flickered on top of a stool right in the middle of the bungalow. An attractive woman sat on one of the platforms. She wore a sky blue Banarsi sari, and she looked no older than eighteen. No praise would be enough for her beauty and delicacy. But at that moment, her wide eyes were wet, and her rosy cheeks were stained by pearly tear drops. On her dainty wrists she wore dark bracelets with elegant inlay work. She held a handsome young man's waistband with her left hand, and with her right hand she held on to his wrist. While she sobbed, he looked at her with a smile. It appeared that he wanted to leave, but her delicate hands restrained him. He appeared to be less than twenty-five, and apart from being handsome, he exuded a dashing and large-hearted nature. His expensive-looking dress went well with his muscled and toned body.

"No! I won't let you go!" the woman said.

"Darling," the man said, "look, don't stop me. If I don't go, people will taunt me. They will say that Birsingh got scared and backed off from arresting a cruel bandit. The King will have a lower opinion of me, and my reputation will be stained."

"That's as may be. But won't they say that Tara knowingly sent her husband to his death?" the woman asked.

"You shouldn't say that—you, a brave man's wife!"

"I do not want to stain your name," Tara said. "On the contrary, I want the pleasure of having the public praise your courage. But it's a pity you forget those things that I have mentioned often to you, the reasons for my fear. I only want you to take me with you, and save me from the clutches of this unjust king. There is no doubt that he has evil designs, and that is why he has pitched you against a bandit who never battles his enemies from the front and instead takes lives by stealth."

Birsingh mulled Tara's words, and said, "I feel certain of your safety as long as your father, Sujan Singh, is around."

"You are right," Tara replied. "I have faith in my father. But when I think of the bowl full of blood that I saw in his hands, my faith gets shaken. All I can think of is that I want to be with you, wherever you are, and stake my claim to an equal half of your fate—whatever it may be."

"Your words strike a chord in my heart," Birsingh said, "and I wish that even if it were against the

King's orders, I could take you with me. But I fear the people who will shake their heads and say 'That Birsingh, he took his wife with him on a fighting campaign!'"

Tara said, "Right. So you think of what they will say, and leave me in the care of my father, in whose hands I saw that silver bowl full of blood…" She shuddered. "God, when I think of it, my heart skips a beat. She was so beautiful…"

"That was evil," Birsingh replied. "I will never forget it. But what choice do we have now? Your father was compelled to… he didn't have the option of refusing." He thought for a while, and then said, "Look, I have a plan."

He sat next to Tara and spoke to her in whispers.

All this time, the man in the grape vines had been spying on the couple with a fixed gaze. He started when he heard footsteps accompanied by the rustling of leaves. He turned around to see another man approaching. "Who is that? Sujan Singh?" he whispered.

"Yes," came the answer. Sujan Singh got close to the man and spoke softly. "Brother Ramdas, if you ordered me away from here, I would remain indebted to you for the rest of my life!"

"Never!" Ramdas said.

"So I will have to kill my daughter?"

"Certainly, if she does not accept."

"How will I do it? My hands are already trembling and I can hardly hold on to this dagger."

"You have no choice!" Ramdas barked softly.

"No—my hands have lost their strength. I will not be able to do it." Sujan Singh pleaded.

"Do I have to remind you of the bowl full of blood?" Ramdas asked in a menacing tone.

Sujan Singh fell trembling at Ramdas' feet. "Oh no, not that dreadful sight! I will do it, the way you have ordered me. If she does not accept, I will kill her with my own hands. But don't talk about that! God, how helpless I am."

"Good," Ramdas said. "We should move towards the gate."

"As you order," Sujan Singh said.

"But wait a minute, maybe these two won't go that way. Yes, look, they have got up. I will follow Birsingh and leave Tara to you."

Back in the bungalow, Birsingh and Tara had finished talking. At this point, we cannot reveal what they discussed, but we can definitely say that Tara appeared happy. Perhaps Birsingh had said something that pleased her, or accepted her conditions.

Birsingh and Tara stood up.

"So I will call your girls and leave you with them," Birsingh said.

"No!" Tara said. "I will come with you to the gate and then go back and meet them."

"As you like," Birsingh said.

They walked hand-in-hand towards the east of the garden, where the gate was. At the gate, Birsingh turned to Tara and said, "This is it. You must go back now."

"When will you come back?" Tara asked.

"I cannot say," Birsingh replied, "but I hope to be back within one watch."

"Go now, and take care. But do not meet the King," Tara said.

"No, never," Birsingh said.

Birsingh walked on. Tara retraced her steps for a while, but then turned south towards a colourful pavilion where some young girls, who looked like servants, were talking to each other.

Tara walked slowly and came close to the grape vines. A man leapt out from the vines, grabbed her and wrestled her to the ground. He sat on her chest.

"Tara," he said in a choked voice, "this is the end. It's no use crying or shouting. I must take your life!"

"Isn't that you, father?" Tara gulped and asked.

"Yes, it is me… Your scoundrel father," Sujan Singh replied.

"Are you ready to kill me yourself?" Tara asked.

"I do not wish to, Tara, but I have no choice!" Sujan Singh replied.

"Is there anyone in this world who would kill his beloved daughter with his own hands?" Tara asked.

"I am such an unfortunate man, Tara! Your sweet voice makes my heart tremble, my eyes grow teary and my throat choke—my dagger slips! My daughter, please just don't say anything."

"Is there no way my life can be spared?" Tara asked.

"There is only one way. You will have to accept the King's condition," Sujan Singh said.

"It's hard to accept it. But what if I do?" Tara said.

"Then you can live. But I do not want you to accept it."

"Of course, I can never accept it. I just wanted to hear you say what you think."

"No, you cannot accept it. Death is a better fate. But what grief! What an unjust act this is."

"Father, my life is in your hands. If nothing else, can you not give me just one chance to see someone?"

"You are mistaken—you will not get to see him. He will leave this world very soon. Perhaps you two can meet in the next world."

"If that is how it is, I am ready to die before my husband. Don't cry, father! And don't delay my death!"

Sujan Singh wiped his tears and said, "Yes, that is how is must be. Now brace yourself!"

## CHAPTER TWO

IRSINGH LEFT THE GARDEN and walked to the road after bidding Tara farewell. Tall *neem* trees lined both sides of the road, and their branches meshed with each other at the tree tops. The canopy of the trees, the moonless night and the clouds covering the stars combined to cover the path in pitch darkness. This did not deter Birsingh. He had walked some distance from the garden when he thought he heard someone following him. He craned his neck and peered back into the darkness, but saw nothing. He moved on, more alert now, as he had an inkling that an enemy was stalking him.

The attack happened soon. A man leapt at Birsingh from his left, and he would have finished

Birsingh off with a thrust of his sword if Birsingh had not been on edge. Birsingh escaped with a scratch, and in an instant he had unsheathed his sword and cried out to challenge his opponent. Unfortunately, his cry brought out two more shadowy men who had been lurking behind the trees a few steps away. Now Birsingh was surrounded by three enemies.

Birsingh was a brave man and his limbs were strong and agile. He had mastered the use of the sword, scythe, gauntlet and dagger. The dullest of swords would shine in his hands, and be capable of vanquishing a couple of men.

At that moment, the three assassins were attacking him from three different directions, but that did not intimidate Birsingh. He coolly parried their thrusts and made his counter-attacks. In a short while, one of his attackers collapsed. Now there were only two of them, and one was showing signs of feebleness. Soon, he retreated and only one fighter remained for Birsingh to combat. This man was a seasoned warrior, and he inflicted many wounds on Birsingh in the next half an hour of their furious duel. Finally, Birsingh's sword detached the man's head from his body, and his torso collapsed to the ground with his limbs twitching grotesquely.

Birsingh had no time to celebrate his victory. He sat below a tree for a short while to recover his breath. As soon as he felt strong enough, he stood up talking to himself: "The matter will not end with these three. There are bad times ahead. I will not

*He did not know whether to feel relieved or horrified*

move forward. I must return—it's quite possible that our enemies have surrounded poor Tara."

With this, Birsingh headed back to the garden where he had taken leave of Tara. When he reached the garden, he went straight to the courtyard where Tara's servant girls and companions were chatting. They stood up when they saw Birsingh approaching, and one of the companions asked him, "Where did you leave sister Tara?"

"I have come here looking for her," Birsingh replied. "I thought she would be with you all!"

"But she was with you," the girl replied. "When did she come here?"

"Oh no," Birsingh muttered.

"What's the matter?" the girl asked. "Where did you leave her?"

"There's no time to discuss now," Birsingh replied. "Get a torch and help me look for her."

Birsingh's words agitated the girls and got them moving. Two of them sprang away and returned soon with two burning torches. Birsingh took those two girls and a few others with him and they started to scan the garden.

The search party reached the grape vines. Birsingh was shocked to see a corpse on the ground. The first chilling thought that flashed in his mind was that it must be Tara. One of the girls brought her torch closer to the corpse, and Birsingh examined it carefully.

He did not know whether to feel relieved or horrified when he saw that the corpse was of a boy who could not have been more than ten years old. The head was missing, but the clothes on the body were opulent. There was a diamond-studded bracelet on the right hand, and the fingers bore many rings. A pearl necklace lay on the ground near the corpse's neck.

Birsingh spoke in a quavering voice, "Even without the head, I can see from the jewels and clothes that this is Prince Surajsingh's body."

"What is this about? Why did the prince come here, and who has killed him?" one of the girls blurted out.

"This is a tragedy," Birsingh said. "There is no way we will escape with our lives when the King hears that the Prince's body was found in Birsingh's garden. I will of course be judged to be the murderer. I will not be able to prove my innocence, and my enemies will have a field day." He turned pensive. "My relatives will also end up hanging. Oh God, is this any reward for a man who has always walked the path of virtue?"

Each of us treasures his or her life, dear reader—and only the one who is useful in a crisis is a true human, relative or friend. The sight of the Prince's body and the distraught Birsingh was enough to make the girls sidle away. Some of them made the excuse that they would still look for Tara, and a few others were cunning enough to pretend that they were searching for hidden intruders. Some did not even bother to pretend—they just melted away. Had it been some other corpse, there might have been a chance of survival. But it was the King's son. Who knew how many would be killed in retribution? Had it been a group of men, a couple of them might have stayed back, but those women did not have such brave hearts. Birsingh was left standing there, alone and forlorn. He stood there for half an hour, lost in thought. Finally he picked up the body and strode to a less trodden part of the garden that had dense, intertwined trees.

Once he got to that deathly quiet place, Birsingh placed the body on the ground. He then walked to the corner that housed the thatched huts of the gardeners. Streaks of lightning lit up the sky, and it started to drizzle.

Inside one of the huts, Birsingh found a gardener in deep sleep. There were a few shovels and picks in a corner. Birsingh took a shovel and stepped out towards the spot where he had left the body. It had started to pour now, and the night was completely dark. Birsingh would have found it hard to retrace his steps if it was not for the short flickers of lightning.

Birsingh felt a deep loyalty to his master, the King, and the Prince, and he had only wanted to bury the Prince's body as a stopgap arrangement while he could trace the Prince's murderer. But try as he did, he could not find the body. He grew increasingly flustered as he continued his search. When the flashes of lightning illuminated the terrain around him, he could have sworn that he was at the very spot where he had left the body. But it had vanished without a trace.

Birsingh felt a numbness creeping over him as he groped around in the slush. The sinking feeling that there was no hope for his life if he could not find the body enervated him, and he wondered how he would get the strength to find Tara.

By this time, Birsingh's clothes were dripping wet and he felt thoroughly bedraggled. Suddenly, a light appeared at the gate, and started to approach him. When it got closer, Birsingh made out that there were actually two burning torches. A group of men had sheltered themselves and the two torches under oil-cloth umbrellas.

Birsingh considered his options, and quickly decided to walk towards them. There was a trophy hall behind the pavilion. He stepped into it and peeled off his wet clothes. He had not yet finished putting on a set of dry clothes when the group reached the pavilion.

Birsingh walked out wearing only a dry *dhoti*. The men bowed and saluted him. Birsingh scanned their faces. Two of them were the King's men, and the others his trusted servants. Birsingh enjoyed a good standing in King Karansingh's court, and the men were bound to be deferential to him. We will reveal more about Birsingh's stature, sociability and integrity as this story unfolds.

"What made you come this way in this dark and stormy night?" he asked.

"The King has sent for you," one of the men said.

"Do you know why?" Birsingh asked.

"Yes," the man replied. "The King has heard bad news about the Prince."

"Bad news?" Birsingh was startled. "What is it?"

"That he has lost his life," the man said with a sigh.

Birsingh found himself trembling. "Is that so?"

"Yes, Sir."

"I will come with you," Birsingh said.

Birsingh went back to the trophy hall and finished dressing himself up. Of course, none of the servant girls was around to help. We think it is belabouring the point to write about how troubled Birsingh was. The reader will definitely understand what a time of torment it was for poor Birsingh, who was deprived of the chance to even get a clue about Tara, whom he loved more than his own life.

Birsingh started off with the group of men. It had stopped raining, and there was less than a watch remaining of the night. As Birsingh and the group walked towards the palace, Birsingh was beside himself with more than one worry. He followed the King's men mechanically, letting himself be guided by the torch lights.

He wondered about Tara—where had she vanished? What trouble had ensnared her? And then there was the inconceivable case of the Prince's corpse. When he thought of the events around the corpse, he feared the worst for himself and his relatives. He trembled at the thought of losing his life in disgrace. It was a completely different matter for him to put his life at stake in battle. He was also chagrined at the infidelity of the fortune, and the thought of the servant girls' mass desertion made him gnash his teeth. It also crossed his mind that the King must have had a very special reason to send so many men with the summon. He consoled himself with the explanation that the King must have been overwhelmed by the loss of his son, and must have been in a nervous state when he ordered ten men to fetch him.

Birsingh pondered all this as he followed the King's men. They were close to the grape vines when the torch bearers came to an abrupt halt.

"Sir! Look, there is a dead body here!" one of them called out.

Birsingh went along with the men to the front of the procession. He was stunned to see the headless corpse lying on their path. It took no time for the King's men to recognise it. Birsingh's mind was reeling from this turn of events. From this very spot, he had picked up the body and taken it to a quieter part of the garden with his own hands; he had searched frantically for it everywhere. And here it was again!

The King's men gave vent to their grief with shouts and tears. The commotion woke up the gardeners, who joined the grieving when they reached the spot.

Birsingh lifted the Prince's body with both hands, and led the group toward the fort with a heavy heart.

## Chapter Three

THE MORNING HAD DIMLY LIT UP the sky by the time Birsingh reached the fort. He still had the Prince's body in his arms. The inhabitants of the fort were in slumber, except for a few elders. Only the King's employees had spent a worried and restless night. As Birsingh and his group walked on, they joined him, and the procession had swelled to fifty men when Birsingh reached the threshold of the audience hall. As soon as he stepped inside, though, the hangers-on made themselves scarce and only ten-odd men remained with Birsingh. News of the Prince's death spread like wildfire, and the city went into mourning.

King Karansingh sat on his throne inside the audience hall. Two recesses had lights and a couple of candles also lit the hall. Birsingh stepped forward till he was right in front of the King. He laid the Prince's body on the ground and knelt and wept, banging his hands against his forehead.

The King recognised the body in an instant, and his grief and anger showed through as he wept with his head bowed, his whole frame convulsing and his fists clenched tight. The courtiers raised laments and smacked their heads as a ritual of grief.

We do not wish to waste words on the state of mourning that prevailed, and the sorrow that the King and his Queen felt. It is enough to say that a full hour passed before the King was able to ask about the Prince's death and where his body was found.

It was only with a visible effort that the King steeled himself and engaged Birsingh in conversation.

"Who killed my son?" he asked in a choked voice.

"Your majesty, we do now know yet who is responsible for this vile act," Birsingh said.

The King looked at one of the men. "Hari Singh, do you know anything about it?"

"Nothing at all, Sir," Hari Singh replied. "But I can say that when we went to call Birsingh, we did not find him at home. We stepped out in the lashing rain to search for him in his garden, and found him there. He was drenched and undressed when he met us. We assume that he was about to change when we got there. We announced your order to him, and he dressed quickly and joined us. By that time, the rain had stopped completely. As we walked through the

*The needle of suspicion points towards Birsingh*

garden, when we got to the grape vines—we found the body!"

The King thought for a while. "We hesitate to say such a thing, because Birsingh is known to be good, honest and kind… But from what you say, we find that the needle of suspicion points towards Birsingh."

# Chapter Four

THREE NIGHTS LATER, in Birsingh's garden, a tall man clothed in black strode up and down near those same grape vines. The garden was forlorn; the courtyard that had echoed with the chattering of girls was silent. Not a single lamp was lit in the complex, which had been adorned with bright lights not so many nights ago. The man walked from the grape vines to the courtyard and onwards to the trophy hall behind it, and back. At the slightest rustle, he would melt into the darkness behind a tree or a shrub.

The man continued to pace that part of the garden fretfully for two hours. Finally, another intruder announced his presence with his footsteps.

The tall man hid behind a tree and surveyed the direction from which the footsteps approached. The intruder walked into the court-yard, stopped for a while and then continued into the trophy hall. In only a little while, he had come out with a small box in his hand. He headed for the gate. He had taken a few steps when the tall man, who was crouching and ready to attack, pounced on him from behind. The tall man held his hands in a tight lock, threw him to the ground and mounted his chest. "Who are you?" he asked. "What brought you here, and what is this that you are taking away?"

The thief found himself breathless and flummoxed. He lay there panting. "Tell me now," the tall man hissed, "or I will strangle you!" His fingers closed in on the pinioned man's throat.

"I am Birsingh's servant, Shyam Lal," he croaked. "The master sent me to get his seal, and that is all I am taking. What is wrong with that? You have no right to—"

The tall man punched him in the face. "You bastard! What is wrong, you ask? Do you know who I am?" He paused for a bit. "That's right, how would you know? If you knew, you wouldn't lie to me. I knew the minute you opened your mouth that you are no servant of Birsingh's. You work for that dishonest Raja Karansingh, who has hatched a foul plot. Your name is Bacchan Singh. I could give you a death penalty myself, right now, but no—I will use you to send a message to that man Karansingh. Listen, and listen carefully: I am Naaharsingh. I am the one whose name sends a shiver down your Raja's spine and makes all of Haripur's citizens tremble. It was my head that the Raja ordered Birsingh to get. And the poor man had hardly left when he was trapped with a false charge." He snatched the box with the deal. "Go tell the Raja that Naaharsingh confiscated the seal. Tell him he is a fool if he sends his army to search for me. Where will he search? Naaharsingh is in this very city. He comes and goes as he pleases. Tell him to watch out; tell him his death approaches. Naaharsingh knows about the bowl full of blood!"

"Bowl full of blood?" Bacchan Singh squeaked. "What is that?" Naaharsingh punched him again, and he squealed in pain.

"This is what!" Don't ask questions. Just give the King my message. And tell him that if I have time, I will drop by eight days from now, on Saturday. Go now—oh, and one more thing. Tell him to keep the Prince safely locked up, unless he wants to be exposed for the fraud that he is."

Naaharsingh released Bacchan Singh and disappeared into the darkness. Bacchan Singh lay there trembling for an hour. When he finally got up, he set off for the palace with unsteady steps. The palace was about a mile away. Dawn was less than two hours away when Bacchan Singh crossed the steps leading to the audience hall. He stood crestfallen, with his hands joined in a namaste, before the King who was waiting for him. A few lamps cast a faint light in the hall. The King sat on a high brocaded throne that was surrounded by strings of pearls. Two men sat on either side of the King, and there were sheaves of papers and an inkpot and pen in front of him.

Now, the reader will ask why the King's demeanour did not reflect the loss of his son. Well, the fact is that in those days, Kings did not cremate their family members themselves, and nor did they shave their heads and observe mourning. In fact, some royal families still have such customs. And then in this case, the matter of the Prince's death was quite curious, as we shall see later.

Bacchan Singh stood there with his head hung low. He was still trembling.

"Did you get the seal?" the King asked.

"Sir, I did get it…" Bacchan Singh said. "But… But Naaharsingh snatched it away from me."

"Naaharsingh?" the King asked, alarmed.

"Yes, Sir," Bacchan Singh replied.

"Is he in the capital?"

"Yes, Sir. He was in Birsingh's garden."

"Tell me clearly, what happened?"

Bacchan Singh narrated the story of his encounter with Naaharsingh, and spoke out Naaharsingh's messages in a tremulous voice.

The King received the message with a stony silence. After a while, he sighed, and said, "This Naaharsingh has troubled me no end, and has evaded arrest all these years. If I free myself of this matter with Birsingh, I am sure I can work out a new plan to arrest Naaharsingh. How does he find out about my activities?" He looked at Hari Singh. "What do you have to say about that?"

"Your majesty," Hari Singh said, "when it comes to this man, my brain fails me. What else can I say?"

"Hmm, that's a pity," the King said. "If Birsingh wasn't so popular, I could have quickly executed him and closed that chapter. I can't be at peace while he lives. Anyway, we do have a serious charge against him now. I will call a session of the court day after, and sentence Birsingh. Then I'll be free to deal with that bastard bandit. He is a nobody."

"True enough, he is a nobody!" a voice rang out from a corner near the door. "But he is a ghost who haunts you and knows you inside out. Look, I am here now!"

The King's jaw dropped, but he was only stunned for a few moments. Then his courage asserted itself. He unsheathed his sword and dashed towards the door, with the two servants following him. It was completely dark at the doorway, and they stopped short of plunging into the dark.

"The scoundrel made it pitch black," one of the men muttered.

# Chapter Five

OOR BIRSINGH WAS ROTTING IN JAIL. His cell was in the basement of a jail about a mile from the fort. The walls of the jail were strong and solid. Birsingh's cell was dark even in the day. People knew his cell as the house of death. Only those destined for the gallows, or death by torture, were kept in that cell. Many prisoners had wept themselves to death there.

Fifty guards were stationed at the entrance to the jail. Five heavy doors with giant locks stood between this entrance and Birsingh's cell.

It was Birsingh's fourth day in his cell. The intense darkness had reduced him to a helpless state in which he had forgotten the way to the door. He

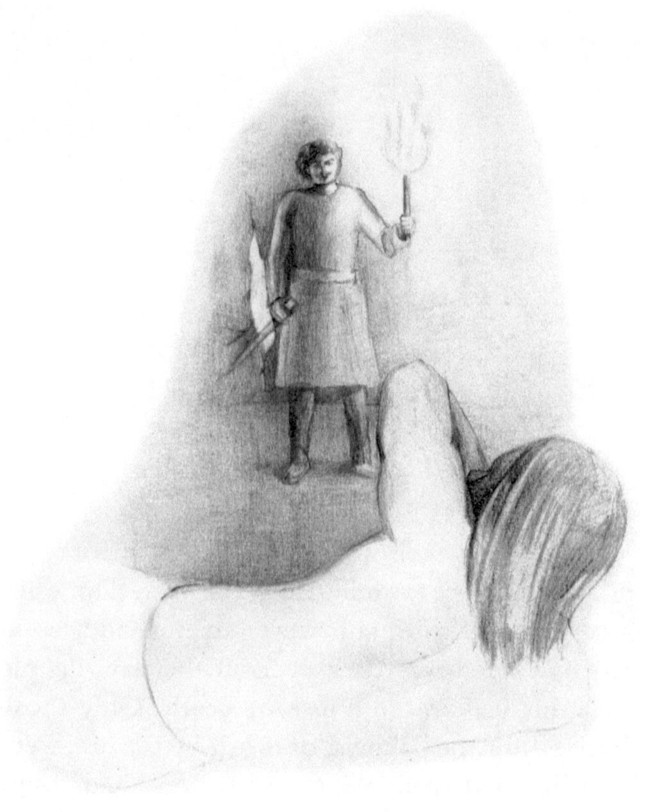

*A tall masked man in black clothes stepped
into the cell with a torch in his hands*

had a feeling that he would not find one hand with the other. Birsingh was racked by thoughts of his innocence, his memories of Tara and his impending death.

He had only been offered dry chickpeas and tepid water, but he had turned them away. He lay on the floor in silent prayer. He did not even know whether it was day or night.

A knocking sound from one of the walls startled him. He sat up, hoping that it was a guard with food and water—but he soon realised that it was someone chipping at the wall of the cell. A dim light flooded the cell and blinded him. It took a short while for a gaping hole, about two fists wide, to appear in one of the walls.

As Birsingh peered at the opening, a tall masked man in black clothes stepped into the cell with a torch in his hands.

"I have come to free you," the tall man said. "Get up, and follow me."

"Before you free me," Birsingh said, "I want to know who you are and why you do me this favour."

"There is no need to discuss these two things right now. We have very little time," the tall man said. "I will tell you about myself once we are out of here. For now, I can tell you that I have come to free you knowing that you are innocent."

Birsingh said, "Everyone knows that I have been proven guilty of the Prince's murder. What makes you think I am not guilty?"

"I know very well that you are innocent," the tall man replied.

"Even so, even if I escape, how will I save myself from the King's forces?" Birsingh asked.

"I have made arrangements," the tall man answered.

"If you have taken so much trouble for me," Birsingh said, "can you also make arrangements so that I can freely roam the city? I ask because my flight from the city will give people all the more reason to suspect me."

"I assure you I have thought through all this. Not only do you not have anything to fear on this count, I can also tell you that you do not need to worry about Tara."

Birsingh's jaw dropped. He said, "Are you a god? Your words make me incredibly happy!"

"I have spoken enough," the tall man said. "I order you to get up and follow me."

Birsingh winced as he stood up with an effort. He followed the man into a narrow tunnel. He figured that the tunnel ran below the foundations of the jail.

When they stepped out of the tunnel into daylight, Birsingh saw that four sturdy men were stationed at the mouth of the tunnel. They greeted the tall man with respect. The group of six walked without stopping for an hour, till they came to the bank of a narrow river. Eight men sat ready to steer a small boat with oars. Birsingh followed his companion's orders and got into the boat. The boatmen steered the boat into the current and it headed downstream. Birsingh took the opportunity to study his fellow travellers. The tall man removed his mask with a flourish and said, "Birsingh! Look at me! And remember me well!"

Birsingh studied the face of the man who had delivered him freedom. By this time, not much remained of the night. Birsingh could make out every detail of the tall man's appearance.

The man must have been about thirty-five. He was fair, and lean but well-built. His face was a bit long, and he had short curly hair. His forehead was wide, his eyes big and his nose long. His moustache seemed soft and proudly curled upwards. His teeth were intact and healthy, and his lower lip was a bit thick. His throat was deep and his chest wide. With his long arms, solid wrists and muscular biceps, he showed evidence of staying strong and fit through exercise. Birsingh was impressed by his looks. We can even say that he was more handsome than Birsingh, but let us first see whether hearing the man's name dampened Birsingh's admiration for him.

"I cannot praise your kindness enough," Birsingh said. "You have done for me what a true brother would have done. Now, Sir, please do me the favour of revealing your name."

The tall man said, "My name is Naaharsingh."

Birsingh's eyes widened. "Naaharsingh… The bandit!" he said.

"Yes," Naaharsingh replied.

Birsingh glanced at the men on the boat, and then looked at Naaharsingh. He said, "But you do not look like a cruel bandit. I think you must be someone else."

"No, no," Naaharsingh said. "I am very much Naaharsingh the bandit. But I am only cruel to the King and his men. The King had ordered you to arrest me, right?"

"That's right," Birsingh said. "But right now I am at your mercy."

"Don't look at it that way. If you had proceeded to encounter me as the King wanted, and we had met in different circumstances, I would still have stood before you and talked to you as I am doing now. Birsingh, you do not know what a scoundrel this King is. You will undoubtedly say that he is the one who brought you up, and gave you a high post. Actually, he did this not out of affection, but out of compulsion. Trust me, he is your mortal enemy. You may not believe me right away, but I know you will soon see the truth in my words."

Birsingh thought for a while. Then he said, "There is no doubt that he does not have all the virtues of a King. But I do not see any evidence that he only helped me because he had no choice."

"It's a pity you don't understand how cunning he is, even though the case of the Prince's body must still be fresh in your mind."

"What do you mean?" Birsingh asked.

"Well, you will figure that out later. Right now, I need to know if you think you can trust me—and look, don't lie to me. Just talk straight."

Birsingh looked into Naaharsingh's clear eyes and said, "I assure you that after what you did today, I am your slave. But truly, I will only consider you a true friend or a brother if I see proof that the King has an axe to grind with me."

"And I assure you," Naaharsingh said, "that I might even prove to you today that the King is your enemy, and that he is using your father-in-law, Sujan Singh, to ruin you."

"That is incredible!" Birsingh said.

"You will find it credible enough when Tara proves it to you," Naaharsingh said. "God willing, she has escaped alive from Sujan Singh."

"Escaped alive—from Sujan Singh!" Birsingh exclaimed.

"Yes, Tara's father has become the biggest threat to her life. And you don't have a clue of the machinations the King has set off to target the lives of three men whom he wants dead."

Birsingh pondered all this. "Sir, how do you know so much? I had heard that you roam the Tarai region of Nepal, where the King had ordered me to seek you out."

"Well, that is what the rumour mills say, that I am in the Tarai. But no—I have no address. And no one can arrest me. Anyway, tell me this: do you even know who you are?"

"Yes," Birsingh replied with a frown. "The King told me that my father was his good friend, and was killed by bandits in the jungle. The King took pity on me and brought me up like his son."

"Lies!" Naaharsingh said. "That's a pack of lies." He eyed the shore. "We will have to disembark close by."

While Naaharsingh and Birsingh talked, the boat went as fast as an arrow, powered by the strong oarsmen. Soon, Naaharsingh ordered the men to take the boat to the shore. Two men jumped off it before it hit the sandy bank. Naaharsingh took a sword from one of the men and gave it to Birsingh. "You may need this," he said.

At that very moment, Naaharsingh noticed an earthen pot floating in the current. He watched it with a keen eye for a while. "There is someone below that pot," he said to Birsingh.

"For sure there is," Birsingh said. "Will you get him?"

"Yes!" Naaharsingh said.

"Or should I take the boat there?" Birsingh asked.

"No, let's leave the boat here. I'll handle this." Naaharsingh took off all his clothes except for his loincloth. He left his sword by his side, but tucked a dagger at his waist and plunged into the water after giving his men a sign. His head bobbed up and down twice before he reached the pot, and then the water became frothy with the two men wrestling each other. The oarsmen quickly steered the boat to the spot, and dragged out the man who had been using the pot to hide his head while floating along the current. The group assembled at the bank, and Naaharsingh's men threw the captive at his feet. He lay there breathless and panting, not daring to look up.

*The water became frothy with the two men
wrestling each other*

Naaharsingh pulled his head up by the hair, and nodded. "It's you, Ramdas, you bastard! You were playing hide and seek, were you? You've met Death now, do you know? Know who I am?" He lowered his voice, but his gaze became steely. "Naaharsingh."

Ramdas pulled back in terror. He was too stunned to react as Naaharsingh searched him. He found a letter wrapped in oilcloth and a dagger, and set them aside. In a few minutes, he had trussed up the quivering Ramdas. "Take him to Nahargarh and imprison him. I will be there the day after, and then I'll see what to do with him."

The boatmen pulled the boat away quickly, and soon it became a small speck. Naaharsingh and Birsingh were left on the river bank.

## CHAPTER SIX

AAHARSINGH READ THE LETTER he had gotten from Ramdas. This is how it went:

*Dear Friend,*

*I have despatched Birsingh to jail on the charge of murdering my son. He will hang soon, and I will sleep better after that. I have made sure my subjects will not resent Birsingh's death. It has taken much time to reach this satisfactory state of affairs. I still have not figured out why the public has a soft spot for Birsingh, and why there is talk of installing him as King. Anyway, my solution will silence the public. Yes, Naaharsingh is still a thorn in my flesh. He has harassed me no end. I hope*

*you can get him out of the way, just as you have so kindly
disposed of Birsingh. Do think of a plan.*

*Your true friend Karansingh*

Birsingh was stunned. He craned his neck to
read the letter again, and then said to Naaharsingh,
"Now I know Karansingh is a very dishonest man.
Until now, I thought of him as a father figure and I
struggled to keep a place in my heart for him. I have
never dreamt of harming him—I do not know why
he should harbour this enmity towards me. To think
that I considered him a benefactor…"

"It is not your fault," Naaharsingh said. "You do
not know who you are, and who Karansingh is. When
you hear that Karansingh killed your father, you will
want that bastard to be thrown to the dogs."

"Karansingh killed my father?" Birsingh asked.

"Yes," Naaharsingh nodded.

"When… why?" Birsingh frowned and shook his
head.

"It's a long story and I can't tell it now,"
Naaharsingh said. "Look, morning has broken—the
red sun is rising there, in the East. We cannot stay. I
assume you will treat me like a brother and spend a
couple of days resting at my place. You will get to know
all the secrets that have been kept hidden from you.

"There is no doubt that I can trust you," Birsingh
said. He thought for a while, and continued in a
pensive tone, "I worry about Tara. I wish I knew
what happened to her."

Naaharsingh said, "I promise I will unite you with Tara, and with your sister, who has become a bag of bones."

"My sister?" Birsingh's mind reeled.

"Yes, you have one," Naaharsingh said with a grim smile. "But like I said, this is not the time to talk. Let us go. We will see what fate God has in store for us."

"Do you know whom Karansingh sent that letter to?" Birsingh persisted.

"Yes, I do indeed. He is another scoundrel whom I will not spare."

They started walking. In his weakened state, Birsingh struggled to keep up with Naaharsingh. About a mile away, they came to a large banyan tree. Birsingh saw two gleaming horses below it. The horses were saddled and brushed.

"I gave orders to have them ready for us before I left to get you," Naaharsingh said with a smile. "That one is yours. Let's go."

They mounted the horses and rode off towards Nepal. Tired and hungry as they were, they did not stop. Only a watch was left of the day when Naaharsingh led Birsingh into a dense jungle. A little later, they came to a ruined building, and Naaharsingh signalled a halt.

Birsingh saw that the run-down house was in a large clearing of about ten thousand square yards. Though it was falling apart, Birsingh could tell that it would easily have hosted more than a hundred people in better times. Its solid, thick walls suggested that it had been built by a King, and Birsingh got the feeling that it must have been decked like a newly-wed bride when it was in use. Most of the insides had crumbled, but some rooms and verandas remained intact. Naaharsingh and his men evidently used these. Birsingh counted some fifty warrior-like men in Naaharsingh's force.

Naaharsingh took Birsingh into a room that seemed to be reserved for his personal use. He told Birsingh to rest for a watch and recover his strength.

## Chapter Seven

HE NEXT DAY, Naaharsingh and Birsingh sat on the grass outside the building. It was a peaceful sunset. The sun had sunk below the trees, leaving a faint amber glow behind. Wisps of clouds travelled the sky, driven by a gentle breeze. Two peacocks vied to drown out each other's cries, and a cuckoo loudly announced its appreciation of the pleasant spring.

All this did not please the two men, who remained lost in their own thoughts. Birsingh turned to Naaharsingh and said, "Now it is time. You must relate the story of Karansingh, as you promised me last night."

"Yes," Naaharsingh said. "I think it is time." He sighed and continued. "A small landlord of Patna,

by the name of Karansingh, was happy with his
station in life. He lived happily with his wife and
children. He had two sons and a daughter. The
events which I speak of occurred when the elder
son was twelve. As fortune would have it, drought
struck two years in a row, and the crops failed in
Karansingh's estates. There was not the slightest
hope of being able to pay revenue to the King. But
the King showed no mercy. He flatly refused to
reduce the tribute by a single coin, or to defer the
payment by a day. Karansingh's estate was confiscated,
leaving him near-bankrupt. He had to sell his wife's
jewellery to raise five hundred rupees. He had a
trusted servant named Karansingh Rathoo, whom
people sometimes called just Rathoo.

Karansingh gave three hundred rupees to his
wife and left her and his children under Karansingh
Rathoo's guard. He himself left Patna in search of
employment, with two hundred rupees.

"In those days, King Narayan Singh ruled Nepal,
and he was renowned for his noble nature and his
concern for his subjects. Karansingh headed for
Nepal. He presented himself in Narayan Singh's
court, and told the King his story. The King took a
liking to Karansingh. He sensed that Karansingh was
an honest, strong and brave man, and he gave
Karansingh a post in the Nepalese army.

"In those days, there were many bandits who
terrorised the Tarai region. Karansingh volunteered
to arrest them, and the King, pleased with his
initiative, sent him at the head of a force of two

hundred men to deal with the bandits. Within six months, Karansingh arrested the bandits one by one. This enhanced his standing in the court. The King gave him the estate of Haripur, which had a revenue of no less than forty thousand rupees after paying the tax. The King also despatched a collector to Haripur with the brief of collecting the tax and giving the net revenue to Karansingh. He appointed Karansingh as a general of the army. Karansingh sent for his wife and children, and found happiness again.

"Two peaceful years later, the King of Tirhut launched a massive invasion into Nepal. Karansingh showed exemplary courage in battling the invader, expelling him from Nepal and even extracting a small tribute from him. The King of Nepal was so pleased with this outcome that he freed Karansingh from service, and gave him and his descendants the district of Haripur. He issued a decree to the collector to give control of Haripur to Karansingh, and return to Nepal.

"Karansingh's wife passed away after a severe fever just when the family planned to leave Nepal for Haripur. Karansingh proceeded on the journey with his three children and his servant, Karansingh Rathoo.

"Karansingh Rathoo hatched a devious plan. He decided to assassinate Karansingh and use the decree from the King to usurp Haripur. He could rely on having the same name. It was a minor problem that he was seven years younger than Karansingh.

"When Karansingh Rathoo thought about his plan, he saw three obstacles. First, the collector to whom the decree was issued knew the real Karansingh. Second, Karansingh's elder son was about fifteen, and he would definitely be an obstacle. Third, Karansingh himself was a formidable man. When the group was mid-way, they received news that the collector had died. A messenger who was taking the news of this death to Nepal met Karansingh, and Karansingh Rathoo manipulated Karansingh into stopping the messenger and telling him that Karansingh would arrange for the news to be given to the King of Nepal.

"Now Karansingh Rathoo worked furiously to realise his ambitions. He bribed Karansingh's assistants with promises of titles and money. He considered wiping out Karansingh's family, but realised that it was better to kill Karansingh and his elder son. He could then take the younger children with him to gain sympathy. They were very young and would not understand the complicated events of their journey to Haripur. In any case the people of Haripur did not know them. The decree and his name would see him through.

"Karansingh Rathoo poisoned Karansingh to death. Then he took Karansingh's elder son deep into a dense jungle, wounded him and pushed him into a well. He proceeded to Haripur with the rest of the group. He won over Karansingh's younger son with his shows of affection.

*He took Karansingh's elder son
deep into a dense jungle, wounded him
and pushed him into a well*

"Karansingh Rathoo found it quite easy to become master of Haripur. In a short while, he had popularised the story that Karansingh's children were his departed friend's. There were some ugly rumours around him, but Karansingh made sure he regularly sent costly gifts to the King of Nepal and stayed on the King's right side. A little later, the King of Nepal passed away and his nephew took the throne. Karansingh Rathoo became even more confident of his position.

"That Karansingh Rathoo is the King of Haripur. And you were in his clutches," Naaharsingh said. "Now tell me, if I am his enemy, what is wrong with that?"

Birsingh stayed quiet for a while, digesting all this. When he spoke, his voice was soft but firm. "There is no doubt he is scum. To be true to him is to go against God."

"No question about it," Naaharsingh nodded his assent.

"But you did not tell me what Karansingh's son is doing now."

"Do you want to know?" Naaharsingh asked.

"Yes, very much," Birsingh replied.

"You are Karansingh's younger son," Naaharsingh said with a smile. He turned serious and continued, "I do not know about your sister. I kept track of her till last year, but this year she seems to have vanished."

Birsingh broke down, sobbing. Naaharsingh turned grave and placed a hand on his shoulder. With an effort, Birsingh straightened himself.

"But you had told me that you would introduce me to my sister who has become a bag of bones," he said. "Is she the one?"

"Of course she is," Naaharsingh said.

"Then what do you mean you don't know where she is?" Birsingh asked.

"I mean that I don't know where exactly she is. My sources tell me that she is in one of the cells in the basement of the fort, and that she is being tortured in the worst ways possible. I had plans to trace her, in fact, but then I heard about you and it became necessary to rescue you."

"What is her name?" Birsingh asked.

"Sundari."

"Do you hope to trace her now?"

"Yes, certainly."

After a few moments of thought, Birsingh said, "There is one more thing I want to know."

"And what is that?" Naaharsingh said.

"Why are you doing all this, and incurring the King's wrath for us?"

Naaharsingh looked into Birsingh's eyes and took a deep sigh. He stood up and paced about for a while. He seemed to be carefully choosing his words. "Yes, it is time for you to know... First, get up and give me a hug."

Birsingh came closer and they held each other.

"I am your elder brother, the one Karansingh Rathoo pushed into a well. God saved me through a merchant who strayed and got there soon afterwards. My real name is Vijaysingh. I live to inflict revenge on the King. I only rob the King—I am not a robber of the common man."

Birsingh was ecstatic. He hugged his long lost brother again. The two brothers walked into the ruined house hand in hand.

# Chapter Eight

T WAS PAST MIDNIGHT, and heavy rain lashed an empty street. Flashes of lightning provided the only respite from a pitch-black darkness, and rolls of thunder punctuated the drumming of the rain. One man braved this downpour. In one hand, he carried a small boy of three wrapped in a blanket, and in the other, an oil-cloth umbrella. He walked towards the fort with purposeful strides. Where he found shelter along the street, he would make use of it for a while. He did not seem to hesitate before stepping into the rain again.

When he reached the field in front of the fort, he turned left towards a high Shiva temple. He strode into the temple and stopped in the main hall to rest for a while. The boy chose that moment to burst into a wail. A huddled shape in one corner morphed into a man. It was the priest, woken up by the boy.

"Who is it? Babusahab?" the priest asked in a bleary voice.

"Yes," came the reply.

"You did well to come. It is a bad time, which means that it is a good opportunity for you," he said.

Babusahab patted the boy and consoled him in a whisper. "It's inconvenient for the boy," he said.

"True, but it is worth it. You've arrived. Follow me," the priest said.

The temple had a common wall with the fort. Truth be told, that fort was not as magnificent as one would expect a fort to be. It was just a huge building, but it did have very thick walls. It had many small cells in its basement. Karansingh Rathoo ruled his small dominion from this fort, and he was a cruel King. He was fond of hoarding wealth and adding to his buildings. To save money, he made do with a minimal army and used the backing of the King of Nepal to control his fief. Naaharsingh was the one threat to this King, and the biggest drain on his treasury.

The priest covered himself with a blanket and stepped out into the pouring rain. Babusahab followed him. They headed for a secret door in the rear wall of the fort. The priest knocked thrice at the door. An unseen hand opened the door from inside, and they stepped in. They saw that the man who had opened the door was a wizened old sentry.

He shut the door immediately. The priest said to Babusahab, "Go now, and come back soon. I will not stay here."

Babusahab left his umbrella on the ground and walked to the small hall to his left with the boy clutched to his chest. He walked through the hall to a room, and then through a courtyard, up a flight of stairs to a roof. Two girls waited for him there. The girls signalled him to follow them. They went down another flight of stairs to a small room.

One of them said, "Now we need old man Ramdin to get us to the basement. We had to do a lot of convincing to get him ready today. The poor man is a kind soul. Our efforts wouldn't have worked with anyone else." The girls left Babusahab alone for a while, and returned with Ramdin.

Ramdin must have been more than seventy. He came in carrying a brass lantern and peered at Babusahab.

"Look, Babusahab," he said, "I am following your orders, but you must understand that my reputation is at stake. In a way, I am betraying my master today by letting you go this way. But I say to myself: 'No, Sundari must be pitied.' Thinking of her moves me to tears, and this small boy's condition breaks my heart. There's no doubt that I am in the service of an unjust King. If I didn't need to make a living, I would have resigned by now."

"You are a good man," Babusahab said. May God reward you for your kindness. Don't resign now, or we will lose a pillar of support. Very soon, the right man will take the throne and liberate the people from this cruel King's claws."

"God willing, it will happen," Ramdin said. "Now, Sir, please wait here for about an hour. You have nothing to fear. I will come back after the King leaves—he is in the basement now. There are three ways into the basement. The main gate has been bricked and there is always a patrol around it. The King uses a second door, for which only he has the key. I have the key to a small window, and I let these girls come and go through it."

"I know about that," Babusahab said, "but tell me, in this one hour, isn't it possible that someone will spot me?"

"No, have no fear. No one will come here, and even if this boy cries you have nothing to worry about as this room is soundproof."

Ramdin left with this assurance, and Babusahab got an hour to talk to the two girls. We think it relevant to repeat only a few of their points of discussion, as they are relevant to this story.

"Did the King come here yesterday as well?" Babusahab asked.

"Yes, Sir," one of the girls said, "but she was adamant. If she refuses to give in for another week, there's no doubt she will lose her life. She is also demoralised by the news of Birsingh's arrest."

"But Birsingh has escaped from jail," Babusahab said.

"When?" a girl asked.

"It's been less than an hour," Babusahab replied.

"How did you know?"

"You don't need to know that!"

"Well, anyway, that's good news. Have you ever met Birsingh?"

"Many times. Unfortunately Birsingh does not know who I am. I am very keen to have his friendship, but so far we haven't had a reason to get close. Actually, I think Tara might bring us together."

"And what about yesterday's council meeting? Did anything come of it?"

"Yes, the council meeting did take place. Fifteen major landlords were there, and they concluded that the throne is Birsingh's. If Birsingh stakes his claim and fights for it, they will support him."

"Have you made any arrangements to support Birsingh?"

"Yes, I have—look, Ramdin is here."

Ramdin told them that the King had left, and they could proceed. He opened the lock to a small window in the room. He ushered them past the window and then locked it behind them. He himself stayed on the other side. Babusahab saw a third girl waiting for them with a lamp in her hand. A flight of stairs led to the basement level. They followed the girl with the lamp. The floor below them now felt colder and wet. They reached a small room, where the girl with the lamp pushed a door open. They walked into a courtyard and saw that there was a bracket that held a vessel and a flickering candle. A mat covered the ground, and a woman draped in a thin sheet slept on a bed with

*He just wrapped himself around the woman's neck,*
*without a word*

a mosquito net. Two girls sat at her feet, fanning her. On one side of the bed, there was a brass stand that bore three silver jugs, a tumbler and a bowl. Right next to it was another silver stand, and on it was a small silver bowl full of blood, a lancet and two needles.

The woman on the bed was very thin and weak. She was all bones, but her face signalled that she must have been a beauty at one time. Babusahab went to her side and stood there with moist eyes, the boy in his arms. The woman saw Babusahab and started crying. She made as if to get up, but Babusahab sat beside her.

"No, don't get up," he said. "You are very weak. Is there any limit to this tyrant's cruelty? Look, this is your son in front of you. Go ahead and love him. It should only be a few days before things are set right here."

He got the boy to sit on the bed. The woman made an effort and kissed the boy with tears in her eyes. It was a wonder that the boy did not cry at all. He just wrapped himself around the woman's neck, without a word. Not a soul in the room was left unmoved.

The woman looked at Babusahab and said, "My love, can I count on my life at all? Can I hope that someday, I will feed this boy as he roams about freely? I had hopes from Birsingh, but the King has sentenced him to death."

"Don't worry my love," Babusahab said. "Believe me, by morning this King's happiness will turn to ashes and he will find himself in the clutches of death. Who can harm the man who has the bandit Naaharsingh protecting him? It is already two hours since he rescued Birsingh from jail."

"Naaharsingh has rescued Birsingh?" the woman said. "But he is a bandit! Why would he help Birsingh?"

"You shouldn't believe that propaganda. If you really ask the people of the city, they will tell you that Naaharsingh only robs the King and his men. He has never troubled the common man. I have often heard that he came incognito into the city and gave money to the poor, or threw bags of money to Brahmans who were struggling to put together dowries for their daughters."

"I did hear such rumours, but I did not believe them. Now let's see if he has actually decided to help Birsingh end this King's rule. I have been here for a year without seeing Birsingh and Tara. As it happened, I kept my name secret from Birsingh and everyone else… I did not tell them that this is who I am, my name is Sundari, but this last year of torture… Oh death would be a sweet relief."

Babusahab was quiet. He looked at the bowl of blood. "Yes, this bowl tells me that I will drink a bowl full of someone's blood!" he said.

Sundari embraced the boy again. "Our evil fates inflict themselves on this boy as well!"

"God willing, within this week people will know that you are married and this child is yours."

"Yes, God willing. What news of the council?"

"The council is all charged up now. They are all for Birsingh."

"Do you know anything else about Birsingh?"

"I do know one thing."

"What is that?"

"It is that it was Tara's father who was compelled to kill her!" Babusahab said.

Sundari took a deep breath. "That scoundrel killed my elder brother Vijaysingh."

"Let me tell you something," Babusahab said.

"Tell me," Sundari replied.

Babusahab bent over and whispered something into her ear. Her face lit up. "Is that true?" she asked.

Babusahab placed his hand on Sundari's head and said, "It is. I swear by you."

A girl butted in: "It seems someone is coming this way."

Sundari gave the boy back to Babusahab with a start. "Oh God, this is terrible," she said. "Is there no peace in my fate?"

The door in front opened, and Hari Singh strode in with a naked sword. Sundari and the girls trembled in fear. Babusahab's face fell for a moment, but he recovered soon and smiled with confidence. Hari Singh reached the bed and blurted out in surprise, "Who are you?"

"What will you do with my name?" Babusahab shot back.

"What brought you here?" Hari Singh replied. He glowered at the girls. "You lot—now I know you're a bunch of cheats!"

"Hey, look at me, and talk to me," Babusahab said, leaving the boy to Sundari. "Don't bully the women."

"I don't want to talk to you," Hari Singh said. "I'll arrest you and take you straight to the King. We'll sort things out then."

"You? Arrest me? I don't think you and your King are worth more than crumbs," Babusahab said.

Hari Singh quivered with rage. He leapt forward and attacked Babusahab with his sword. Babusahab sidestepped him with ease, grabbed his wrist and jerked it so hard that the sword fell a few feet away with a clang. Both of them wrestled desperately. Very soon, Babusahab flung Hari Singh to the ground. By chance, his head struck a stone door frame and blood started oozing from the wound. One of the girls jumped to the sword, picked it up and detached Hari Singh's head with a clean blow.

"What have you done?" Babusahab asked.

"He's better off dead, or he would have created a ruckus," the girl said.

"What happened, happened," Babusahab said. "Now all we can do is take him out and bury him and his secret."

Babusahab walked over to Sundari, and after some convincing, got permission to leave. One of the girls took the boy in her arms, and Babusahab tied the dead body to his back after wrapping it in a blanket. The party retraced their steps to the exit. When they got to the window, Babusahab knocked on the door chain. Ramdin was still waiting there. He opened the window in an instant.

Ramdin saw the bundle on Babusahab's back and stepped forward in alarm. "What on earth are you up to? Are you taking Sundari away? No, I can't allow that. I will hang for sure! It's enough that I let you go to her."

Babusahab got the bundle off his back, and opened it. "Don't think that I will bring trouble upon you," he said. "This is someone else who intruded when we were there. I had to kill him to keep my visit a secret, and to protect you all."

"This bastard Hari Singh had been hounding us for ages," a girl said.

"Well," Ramdin nodded, "since he got to Sundari at such an inopportune time, he had to die. Now he has to be buried where he won't be found."

"Don't worry about that," Babusahab said. "I'll take care of it."

We don't feel the need to repeat the details of Babusahab's way out of the fort. In short, he was soon out of the fort, and walking on the plain in front of it. This time, he had a girl holding the boy in her arms and he himself carried the large bundle on his back. It had stopped raining and there were a few stars sprinkled in the sky.

Babusahab walked away from the Shiva temple. He had not walked far across the silent field, when two men with scythes materialised out of the dark.

"Stop there! One of them said. "Put that bundle in front of me, and tell us who you are. That has to be a corpse."

"Yes, it is," Babusahab replied calmly. "And it is the corpse of a man who was a menace to the public.

I don't think there is any one in the kingdom who will grieve for him."

"How do you know we won't?" the man asked.

"Because you don't look like the King's men," Babusahab said.

"That may be so," the second man said, "but whose body is it? And who are you?"

Babusahab lowered the bundle to the ground. "It's Hari Singh's body. But I won't tell you my name without first knowing yours."

"Of course I'm happy to hear that Hari Singh is dead. And I think I can reveal that my name is Naaharsingh. I am guessing that you are on our side, but even if you aren't, I don't need to worry too much about it."

"Naaharsingh! I am delighted," Babusahab said. I have wanted to meet you for a long time, but I didn't know how to get to you. It would be great to meet Birsingh as well!"

"What business do you have with Birsingh?" the second man asked.

"I would tell him that the King is his enemy, that he should worry about the plight of his sister Sundari, of whom he does not even know. I would also tell him that his wife Tara has just escaped, but is fighting for her life…" He trailed off and looked at Naaharsingh. "I know that you have rescued Birsingh from prison, and that you can take me to Birsingh."

"Aha, now I know that you are Babusahab." Naaharsingh said. "Well, not really, but that is how a lot of people know you, right?"

"That's right," Babusahab said.

"I don't know everything about you," the man said, "but I am trying to get to know more. And by the way, this is the right time to let you know that I am not Naaharsingh. We both are his men. But it's true that Naaharsingh has freed Birsingh today, and if you come to his house you can meet both of them.

"I would very much like to do that," Babusahab said.

"Who is this boy with you?" the man who had claimed to be Naaharsingh asked.

"You will get to know all about him when I speak to Naaharsingh," Babusahab said.

"So are you ready to go there now?" the man asked.

"Sure!" Babusahab said.

"Fine then. Give me the body. I will bury it later and just take the head to show the master. Take the boy in your arms, and let the girl go. We have an extra horse with us."

Babusahab sent the girl away, and in a short while, he was riding behind the two men with the boy in his arms. They had not travelled far when they heard the hooves of horses behind them.

"It won't surprise me if those horsemen are out to arrest us," Babusahab said.

# Chapter Nine

T WAS MIDNIGHT. Thick clouds cloaked the stars. Strong gusts of wind blew away a few drops of rain. Haripur was deathly quiet. Two masked men in black walked stealthily in the back alleys. They were clearly in a hurry, but in that darkness, they often had to wait for the occasional lightning flash to show them the way.

They finally reached a palatial house guarded by about a dozen men with unsheathed swords. One of the two stepped forward and said, "Mahadev!"

"Mahadev!" the guards responded.

One of them, who was taller than the others, stepped forward and asked, "So you have company today? Will this gentleman go inside as well?"

"No," was the reply. "I will go alone first, but when the chief calls for him, he will follow."

"That sounds fine," the guard replied.

One of the two visitors stayed back and started strolling about, while the other crossed the threshold. Still masked, he crossed three more doors before he reached a large hall in which about twenty men sat on a carpet, speaking in whispers. Four men at the fringes were fanning the assembly. Two wax candlesticks burned in the centre, and the men sat around them.

Each one of them seemed regal and strong, and was armed with a sword. With their impressive moustaches, broad shoulders and clear eyes, they exuded the air of men who lived by their swords. They wore smart silken jackets and red turbans, and they had red sandalwood *tilaks* on their foreheads. They sat in the warrior pose, in two rows facing each other.

One of them, who sat confidently in the middle, was younger than the others. He had a sword with an inlaid hilt in front of him. His expensive-looking, crisp, silk dress indicated that he was a man of high station, most likely an army officer. His flat nose confirmed that he was from Nepal, and one would conclude that he was the General of the Nepalese army, or at least the head of one of its units.

The masked man walked into this council, and bowed and saluted the braves. He said, "Today I thank the King of Nepal from the bottom of my heart. He has sent a chief to help the people of

Haripur. I am happy to see you, Sir, in this gathering of elders, *Kshatriya* landlords and honourable men. And I request you"— here he bowed again—"to conduct a detailed inquiry into the cruelty that Raja Karansingh inflicts on us. We are ready to prove that Raja Karansingh is a cold-blooded and dishonest tyrant."

The Nepalese chief, Kharagsingh, turned to one of the men at his side and asked, "Anirudhsingh, who is this man?"

"He is a confidante of Naaharsingh, whom Karansingh has branded as a bandit. He often joins our council. His name is Somnath. He has always joined this council incognito. We did not insist that he should reveal himself, and in fact we have promised that we will not betray him." Anirudhsingh replied.

"So you engage with Naaharsingh's man? The same Naaharsingh who has terrorised your people and who is known even in Nepal for his fearlessness and cruelty?"

Somnath intervened. "Karansingh has created this myth about Naaharsingh, because Naaharsingh has always been a thorn in his side. Naaharsingh has robbed the state and freed innocent prisoners from jail. Except for the King's men, not one man in Haripur has a complaint against Naaharsingh.

"Is this true?" Kharagsingh asked Anirudhsingh.

"Absolutely," Anirudhsingh said. "Naaharsingh is, in fact, an honourable and brave man. He has never troubled the people at large, and in fact he donates thousands of rupees secretly to the poor and to Brahmans. It is true that he has killed and robbed the King's forces."

"If all this is true, I can say that Naaharsingh is a principled man," Kharagsingh said, looking at Somnath. "But Karansingh insists that Naaharsingh is an evil bandit, and by way of proof, he points to Naaharsingh's role in the traitor Birsingh's escape—the same Birsingh who was proven guilty of the Prince's murder and was condemned to death by cannon fire. What does Naaharsingh have to say to that?"

Anirudhsingh said, "We have only met Somnath since that accident, and this is a question that even we wanted an answer to. We did not expect this from Naaharsingh. We are against the King, true, but we could not carry our enmity so far as to prevent justice being meted out to the Prince's murderer. On the other hand, we are also perplexed that Birsingh, of all people, committed the act. He is a good soul, and we used to think him to be far superior to the King. He is the one man in the government who treated the subjects like his children, but the surprising thing is that—"

"I can answer the question," Somnath interrupted. "In short, neither has Naaharsingh done anything wrong and nor has Birsingh."

"If they are proven innocent, we will initiate some major actions on their behalf," Kharagsingh said. "Listen, Somnath. The King of Nepal has sent me here in response to petitions he has been getting from the people of Haripur and from Naaharsingh. I will be fair in my enquiry." He signalled to the council. "These people know me well and hold me in high esteem. That is why I could become a part of this secret council. They are frank with me. Now tell me, what do you have to say for Birsingh's innocence?"

"Well, as to who Birsingh is and why you should respect him, I will have more to say at another time," Somnath said. "For now, I will focus on his alleged crime. Birsingh did not kill the boy. The King created a web of deceit to frame Birsingh. The Prince is alive and kicking, and the King has hidden him away. I can take you to the Prince."

"What!" Kharagsingh gasped. The council was stunned.

"Yes, Sir," Somnath said.

"This is enough for me to believe the petitions and arrest Karansingh if it is true."

"Not only this, the King has killed several of Birsingh's innocent relatives. If I tell you the whole story, you will find it hair-raising."

"If all this is true, we are ready to support Birsingh right now. But we need to see Naaharsingh in person," Kharagsingh said with a frown, fondling the hilt of his sword.

At that moment, the men in the council spontaneously unsheathed their swords and swore by their faith to verify the facts, and then support Naaharsingh. The man who had been introduced as Somnath now flung back his mask, held his sword to his forehead and spoke in a resonating voice.

*Kharagsingh got up and embraced Naaharsingh*

"I, Naaharsingh, stand before you and swear that if I am found false, I will behead myself at Durga's feet. I am Naaharsingh. I used Somnath as an alias till today."

The light of the candles shone on Naaharsingh's handsome face. His appearance, voice and demeanour entranced the men. Kharagsingh got up, embraced him and said, "You are doubtless a brave man. Only you could have made yourself present at such a time. If Goddess Bhagvati wills it, you will be found to be a true man." He looked at the rest of the men. "Rise, and embrace this brave man. He will deliver you from the evil regime."

The men rose and made Naaharsingh welcome. Kharagsingh gave him a place of honour next to himself.

"I have left Birsingh waiting outside," Naaharsingh said when they had again settled down.

"Did he accompany you here?" Kharagsingh asked.

"Yes, Sir," Naaharsingh replied.

"Excellent! We have to see him," Kharagsingh said. He looked at one of the chiefs. "Will you get him?"

"Sure," the chief said. He set off for the main entrance, but it was a while before he returned with Birsingh.

"What took you so long?" Kharagsingh asked.

"The gentleman had strolled some distance away," the chief said, signalling towards Birsingh.

"Birsingh, come over and reveal yourself. I have just done it," Naaharsingh said.

Birsingh shook his head.

"What's wrong with you?" Naaharsingh asked. "I just took your name—what have you got to hide now? I thought you were a brave man."

Birsingh again shook his head and took a few steps back. Naaharsingh's nostrils flared with rage. He leapt to Birsingh and grabbed his wrist. As soon as he had done that, he looked at Birsingh from head to toe and said, "This is not Birsingh. The King has tricked us. Birsingh must be in trouble!"

Naaharsingh snatched away the impostor's mask. Many in the council recognised the man who stood cowering before them—it was the King's dear servant, Bacchan Singh.

"What is all this?" Kharagsingh asked.

"This is a trick. This man confidently came here thinking that he would not to reveal himself. I can't say what our enemies have learnt through him. I had caught this scoundrel in Birsingh's garden, when he tried to steal Birsingh's seal. If I had not got in the way, who knows what that devilish King would have done with that seal?"

Kharagsingh stood up, walked to Naaharsingh and said, "There's no doubt we have been fooled. I am sure Karansingh knows quite a bit about this council. One among us is a traitor."

"We will have to figure this out," Naaharsingh said. "Right now we must step out and find Birsingh. We had better keep this villain in custody though."

This sudden turn of events had caused a sensation in the council. The men were all on their feet, and it was clear that their mood had changed to anger. One of the chiefs strode to Bacchan Singh and planted a kick on him. "Tell us where Birsingh is, and what you have done with him, or I will behead you right now!" he shouted.

Bacchan Singh kept mum. The chief who had threatened him, whose name was Harihar Singh, turned to Kharagsingh and said, "Leave this bastard with me. I'll take care of him. Please go find out about Birsingh."

Kharagsingh signalled Naaharsingh closer and asked him in a whisper, "What do you make of this?"

"The same as you," Naaharsingh replied. "This man is too eager, and that makes me suspicious."

"I am sure of it now," Kharagsingh said loudly.

Kharagsingh immediately ordered both Harihar Singh and Bacchan Singh to be taken into custody. "The King's dishonesty is now quite clear to me," he said. "This is not a good time for talk. Keep watch on these two, and we will step out to find Birsingh.

Kharagsingh chose three of his men to accompany him, and said to Naaharsingh, "Let's move fast." The five of them raced to the main gate.

Naaharsingh asked the guards, "Did my friend stay here or go off?"

"He went that way, Sir," one of the guards replied, pointing to his right.

"You see," Naaharsingh said to Kharagsingh, "it's a bit clearer now."

"Let's go on!" Kharagsingh said.

"I feel sorry for Birsingh," Naaharsingh said.

"Don't worry too much. Have faith in me," Kharagsingh said. He got one of the guards to follow them. Naaharsingh masked himself again, and they ran in the direction which Birsingh had taken.

It was not long before they came upon a dead body. The ground around it was soaked in blood.

## Chapter Ten

 NSIDE HARIPUR FORT, King Karansingh sat on his throne conferring with two of his men. The two men stood in front of him with their palms joined in supplication. Their names were Shambhudutt and Saroopsingh.

"I was troubled by Ramdas' disappearance, but Hari Singh's worries me even more."

"Well, Ramdas was sent on a mission, and it's possible the mission hasn't been accomplished. But you didn't even send Hari Singh anywhere," Shambhudutt said.

"All this has to be Naaharsingh's doing," Saroopsingh said.

"I'm sure it is," the King said. "I don't even know what I have done to antagonise that cursed man. He has become a spectre that haunts all of Haripur. He laid waste to many months of our work by rescuing Birsingh. And by snatching Birsingh's seal from Bacchan, he spoiled our plans to completely nail Birsingh."

"True enough, your majesty." Saroopsingh said. But how long will you keep the prince hidden? Isn't there a risk that the secret will leak out?"

"Don't be a fool. The day we will reveal Prince Surajsingh, we will also repent for our mistake and mourn Birsingh for months. But we have to get hold of that Birsingh first."

"Birsingh is very popular. People don't believe that he murdered the prince," Saroopsingh muttered.

"Well that is why we needed the seal, but it did not work out," the King said.

"In fact, the people are quite upset," Shambhudutt said. "Among the landlords, only poor Harihar Singh supports you in the council. If you don't do something about all this, the council will turn against you."

"What do I do? If I had snuffed out Birsingh without good enough reason, I would have faced a revolt. Ah, that Naaharsingh! He is the root of all our troubles. On the other hand, if I had finished Birsingh off when he was a child, I wouldn't have been in this state today. How could I have known that he would be so popular among my subjects? He has them eating out of his hand. Now Kharagsingh has come down from Nepal to conduct an enquiry. Let's see how he does it. I know from Harihar that the council has already won him over."

"Oh we will get to know every detail of today's council meeting," Saroopsingh said.

"Bacchan Singh has taken a force of twenty-odd men there. Let's see what he gets done," the King said.

"Kharagsingh has an army of four hundred men. If it was just a couple of men, we could have sorted them out," Saroopsingh said.

The King laughed, and said, "Do you think we will spare them? Forget the King of Nepal, even Kharagsingh's aides will never figure out what happened when I strike to finish him off. But first, we should figure out what to do about Sujan Singh."

Their discussions continued till most of the night had passed. Only an hour of darkness remained when the door to the hall was flung open, and four men marched in bearing a corpse.

# Chapter Eleven

OW IT IS TIME for us to tell about Tara, whom we left behind in the first chapter. Tara had given up on her life when her own father Sujan Singh had readied himself to kill her. She had felt hopeless when she heard that Birsingh was destined for a quick death. As it turned out, her death was still far away. Two men appeared on the scene and wrenched Sujan Singh away from her. Sujan Singh turned his knife towards one assailant, but the man countered him with a dagger. The second man easily lifted Tara in his arms, said something in a strange tongue to his companion who was battling Sujan Singh, and ran to the garden gate. Tara screamed and fainted.

When she woke up, she found herself in an ordinary hut. A mild incense fire glowed in the middle of the hut. A sage, who was caked in ash and wore long dreadlocks and a large knotted beard, sat in front on the fire. He watched Tara with a steady gaze.

"Don't be afraid, child," he said. "Take care of yourself, and you will be well soon." His voice was soft and reassuring, and the pounding in Tara's heart slowed down. She was able to bring herself to sit up.

"Is Tara really your name, or am I wrong?" the sage asked.

"It is, Sir," Tara replied with a *namaste*.

The sage stepped to a corner of the hut and picked up two mangoes. He placed them in Tara's hands and said, "First eat these. Then we will talk."

Tara was very disturbed. All kinds of thoughts pummelled her—she feared the worst for Birsingh. The thought that death would relieve her from her troubled state also crossed her mind. She felt no hunger, but the sage insisted that she eat the mangoes. When she stepped out to wash her hands, she saw that the hut was at the bank of a river, and all around was a quiet plain. The sun was past its zenith when Tara had washed up and returned to the hut, where the sage waited for her.

"Now, Tara, I expect that you will tell me the truth about yourself," he said.

"Be assured that I will, Sir," Tara said. "Something makes me hope that you will help me."

"I swear by this sacred fire in front of me that you must only expect me to work for your good.

*"First eat these. Then we will talk."*

Now tell me: who are you, and what troubles you?"

"My father is Sujan Singh, the King's treasurer," Tara said.

"And you are Birsingh's wife?" the mystic asked.

"Yes, Sir," Tara said.

"I know he is your father," the sage said, "but I have to say that Sujan Singh is a selfish man and a traitor by nature. At the same time, Birsingh is brave, capable and concerned for the people. He is a good soul. Now tell me, since you are Sujan Singh's daughter, you must have been a regular visitor to the palace?"

"Yes, Sir. I have spent months there, earlier, but not anymore—these days I do not visit either the palace or my father's house," Tara replied.

"And why is that?" the sage asked.

"Because the King and my father are after my life!" Tara said.

"Well, I will figure that later, but tell me, why does your father tremble at the very mention of the bowl full of blood? What is this secret?"

Tara shuddered. "It gives me the jitters to think about it. It was horrible! I will tell you, but this is a very sensitive matter."

"I have already sworn that you should only expect me to work for your good. Have no fear," the sage said.

"I will tell you. My heart tells me that you wish me well, and I sense only affection in your heart."

Tara's words made the sage's eyes moist. He took a little ash from the fire and rubbed his eyes dry with it. "That is how God wants it. Tell me the secret. I am very curious about it."

"But along with it I will have to tell you a bit about myself," Tara said.

"That is fine. I will hear you out," the sage said.

"Well, it's like this," Tara began. "Since my childhood, I was a regular at the palace. I would spend days on end there. A girl named Ahilya lived there. She was much older than me, but I loved her very much, and she returned my love. I did not know who her parents were, and whether she had any relatives. I asked her about her parents many times, but she would start crying instead of telling me about them. Birsingh and I knew each other when we were very small. He often accompanied the King to the palace, and he usually spent some time with Ahilya, who treated him like a brother. I used to call Ahilya *bibi*, elder sister. Both Ahilya and Birsingh were close to the King, and it was Ahilya who arranged my marriage to Birsingh."

"Did Ahilya have another name as well?" the sage asked.

"For a long time, I thought she only had that one name," Tara said. "Then a dreadful thing happened and I got to know that she had another one as well."

"What is that name?" the sage asked.

"I will tell you, but there's a lot to tell," Tara said.

"Go on then," the sage said with a smile.

"The Queen often suggested to the King that Ahilya was growing into a woman and that she should be married, but the King did not agree. In a few days, it became clear to the queen and her ladies that the King had designs on Ahilya, and that was why he refused to have her married."

"He's a bastard and a scoundrel," the sage said. "What happened next?"

"The Queen was shattered. It led to a few quarrels between the royal couple, but one day the King firmly announced that he would not allow Ahilya's marriage."

"Hmm," the sage frowned. "And then?"

"The King's statement pierced the Queen like an arrow. Ahilya's face turned pale with fear and she shrank back from the King's presence. A few days after this episode, she just disappeared from the palace. The King created a ruckus. He beat up a few of the girls, dismissed some of them and stopped talking to the Queen, but all of that didn't help him to trace Ahilya."

"Is she still not traceable?" the sage asked.

"It's complicated. A few years later, I overheard a girl telling the queen that Ahilya had had a second child, a boy. Her girl was three. She said that her husband, may he live long, was a good man who loved her very much.

"My marriage happened before Ahilya disappeared. Of course, I started living in Birsingh's house. Birsingh and I were angered when Ahilya disappeared, and I reduced my visits to the palace. When I heard the news about Ahilya, I felt happy for her. I told Birsingh about it, and he was also relieved to hear the news. Later, we

*"My father had a small girl of about three in his arms"*

got news that the Queen had sent Ahilya to her father's place."

"Tell me, who else lives in your marital home?" the sage asked.

"It's not much of a household," Tara said. "There are a few couples there that my husband calls uncles and aunts, but they are not actually relatives. My husband's parents passed away when he was a child, and the King brought him up. The King has held him in high regard, but he has always cautioned me that the King is a very dishonest man, and that there is a good chance that someday he will fall out with the King."

"Go on," the sage said with a nod.

"Many days passed, and the Queen summoned me. I went over and stayed for four days. One night, I lay near the Queen in her chamber, with a few of her girls near us. The Queen was fast asleep, and so were most of the girls. Suddenly a whimpered voice carried through to me: 'Poor Ahilya finally got captured. Let's go and see how she is doing. We'll be able to spy on her from the ventilator in the minister's audience hall. She might even be killed tonight. We should also let the Queen know about it later."

"My heart started pounding, and the tension suffocated me. I found myself propelled by a force that made me sit up and then walk to the roof, from where I walked to the portion that would take me to the roof of the audience hall. I stepped over the waist-high boundary between the two buildings.

Through small slats in the roof, I could see the goings-on in the audience hall. Two girls had got there before me."

"Who were they?" the sage asked.

"Oh, they were the Queen's girls," Tara said. "They came to me with joined palms and said, 'Please don't do anything that costs us, and you, our lives—if the King or his men see us, they will not spare us!' I told them not to worry."

"That audience hall was an old one. The King had got a new one made, and this one had fallen into disrepair. No lamps were lit in it, and people had started to fear it as a haunted place. When I looked through the ventilator, I saw Ahilya with her head sunk, weeping disconsolately. Four men stood holding shovels in one corner. In the opposite corner, there were about two dozen pots of water. The King stood right in front of Ahilya, with my father Sujan Singh and his loyal servant Hari Singh flanking him. My father had a small girl of about three in his arms. It gives me goose bumps just to think of the way that poor girl looked. I will never be able to forget it! 'Sundari, will you not listen to me?"

"So you will not be mine?'"

"What name did you say? Sundari?" the sage asked. His forehead was wrinkled and his eyes wide.

"Yes, Sir," Tara said. "That is when I realised she had a second name."

"Oh. And what happened next?" the sage asked softly.

"Sundari shook her head," Tara said.

"And then?" the sage asked.

"The King said, 'Sundari, if you do not give in, you will regret it. Don't think I can't use force with you. All I want is to make you mine forever, and not for once. If you like, I can kill the Queen and make you my Queen.' And Sundari replied, 'You wicked man, even if you came to me in the guise of Lord Indra, I would not change my mind!"

"She spoke well!" the sage said. "What then?"

"The King must have made some kind of sign to my father, who bundled the little girl in a cloth and hung her from a big nail. He stood before her with his dagger drawn and gleaming. The little girl's wails filled the room, and Sundari's tears streamed down her cheeks."

"Sundari, don't be stubborn. There is still time,' the King said. If you don't give in, I will bathe you in your daughter's blood!"

"How can I give myself to you and betray my husband? Sundari asked. No, I can't."

"The King signalled Hari Singh and my father. Harisingh placed a big bowl below the little girl, and my father advanced to kill her. God knows from where a shift of pity entered his heart, and the dagger fell to the ground from his trembling hand. The King unsheathed his sword and swore at him, 'You bastard, did you not hear me? I want this girl's blood in that bowl, and I'll make this mother of hers drink it!'

"My father picked up the dagger and slashed at the girl. A stream of blood spurted out. Sundari cried out in grief and fainted. I myself fainted and fell to the ground. It must have been an hour later that I woke up. This time, however, when I peered groggily through the ventilator, I saw a different scene. Neither Sundari nor that poor hanging girl were there. There were two dead bodies on the floor, and the King and his men stood talking glumly.

"'These two girls were watching us from the roof,' the King said. 'They didn't fear for their lives! Hari, dump them where they won't be found for a thousand years. And you, Sujan Singh, you let Tara get away when these two clearly told you that she was around. Well, you will stay alive only when you bring her head to me. And do it with finesse—not a soul should discover where she disappeared. I expect Tara to reveal what she has seen to Birsingh. Anyway, it is time for me to get rid of that Birsingh as well.' I almost passed out again. I fled the palace with a servant girl and reached home."

The sage's face had turned ashen during the narrative. He stayed quiet for a long time. Then he shuddered and said, "This is an evil and cruel King. But God willing, he will soon meet his fate."

## Chapter Twelve

E HAVE WRITTEN EARLIER that Kharag-singh dashed out of the council meeting with three of his men, and Naaharsingh, in search of Birsingh. The party found a dead man a little distance away. By the light of a lantern, they saw that it was one of the King's men who had died.

"Birsingh must have fought the King's men here," Naaharsingh said.

Kharagsingh said, "It wouldn't surprise me if he was outnumbered and arrested."

"So if we head towards the palace and confront the King, we can free Birsingh," Naaharsingh said.

"I will go. Will you come with me?" Kharagsingh asked.

"Sure! I have no fear, and your support makes me feel invincible. And who recognises me there?"

"That's great," Kharagsingh said. After a pause, he continued, "On second thought, though I salute your courage, I would advise you to stay back for now. The matter is a bit complicated. If Birsingh is there, I will extricate him… But I don't want you to be alone here either."

"Don't worry about me," Naaharsingh said. "I won't be alone. My men are in hiding around here."

"Well, then I will go with these trusted men," Kharagsingh said.

Kharagsingh marched to the palace with his team. The soldiers at the entrance made an effort to stop them, but Kharagsingh brushed them aside. They did not dare to be too assertive, as they knew who Kharagsingh was.

Kharagsingh stormed into the audience hall, and what did he see there but the King conferring with his men Saroopsingh and Shambhudutt, while four other men who must have just got there were laying the badly wounded Birsingh on the ground. Birsingh was clearly holding on to his life by a slender margin.

For a fleeting moment, the King's face betrayed shock and anger at Kharagsingh's sudden appearance. Then he composed himself and said calmly, "Look— my men have been through a lot of hard work and trouble to get my son's murderer back, after that scoundrel Naaharsingh helped him escape."

"I congratulate you on the arrest of the murderer," Kharagsingh said quickly. "My enquiries show that

Birsingh is an evil traitor. I will behead him myself. Oh, and I have to congratulate you for one more thing."

"What is that? the King asked.

"I have also arrested your enemy Naaharsingh!" Kharagsingh said.

The King's face lit up. "Excellent! That is a great task you have pulled off! Where is he?"

"I have sent him under guard to my camp," Kharagsingh said. "I consider it wise that you ask your men to take Birsingh there as well. I will summon a *durbar* tomorrow, in which I will conduct a public hearing. We will confer the title of *Adhiraja* from the King of Nepal on you, and I will put these two to death without much deliberation. By the way, you also have a couple of other enemies. I will also pronounce the death sentence on them."

"How do you know that I have other enemies?" Kharagsingh asked.

"The King of Nepal sent me with clear instructions to assist you, and to seek out and kill your enemies. He told me that the locals are very cunning and scheming, and ordered me to hand you a decree making you *Adhiraja*, to keep the people in check. Following his orders, I engaged with the secret council of landlords and chiefs that conspires against you. That was all I had to do to know who your enemies are."

The King laughed and said, "You have done me a big favour. I couldn't have refused your order anyway, but with this favour you have made me your slave. Can you tell me who those enemies of mine are?"

"I will not reveal the names now," Kharagsingh said. "Tomorrow will be the day when I will expose them and sentence them to death. They will be left wondering how we pierced their secrecy."

In fact, the King was stunned with fear when he saw Kharagsingh striding into the court. He controlled himself with an effort. He realised that he must keep up appearances, even as he decided on the spot that he must get rid of Kharagsingh, stealthily and without leaving a trace.

Kharagsingh was also thinking furiously. He realised that he had been a bit impetuous in storming into the court with only three men. It struck him that the King might even want to get rid of him. He recalled the King had his spy in the council, and the spy must have informed him of Kharagsingh's activities. It had crossed Kharagsingh's mind that the King might even choose that very moment to kill him. That thought prompted him to use his wits, and he had spun a web of words around the King. Kharagsingh's words had the desired effect—the King started to think on the lines that he needed Kharagsingh.

The King ordered his men to take the wounded Birsingh to Kharagsingh's camp. When the party left the court and reached the road, Kharagsingh ordered two of his men to first bandage Birsingh and then go with the others. He took his third companion towards the place where they had left Naaharsingh.

Kharagsingh found Naaharsingh close to the house where the council had convened. Naaharsingh was not alone any more—he had five men with him. "Is that you, Naaharsingh?" Kharagsingh asked.

"Yes, Sir," Naaharsingh replied.

"And who are these men?" Kharagsingh asked.

"They are my men. They were hanging around, waiting to come to my aid."

"Are these all your men, or do you have more?" Kharagsingh asked.

"Oh many more," Naaharsingh said. "I can raise a hundred men in half an hour."

"That's just as well," Kharagsingh said, "because it wouldn't surprise me if we have to go to battle at short notice."

"Did you find out about Birsingh?" Naaharsingh asked.

"Yes, indeed," Kharagsingh said. "Karansingh's men had wounded him and taken him to the palace. But I got there just in time. He couldn't hide Birsingh from me. I have it under control. Birsingh is now being taken to my camp, under the protection of my men."

"And how is he?" Naaharsingh asked.

"Not too bad," Kharagsingh replied. "He is wounded, and he shows signs of having put up a brave and full fight. My men bandaged him. Now let's move fast. The chiefs must be waiting for me."

"That's right, Sir," Naaharsingh said. "They will be worried till we get back."

Naaharsingh followed Kharagsingh back inside the house. The chiefs were still there, and they stood when Kharagsingh entered. Kharagsingh motioned Naaharsingh to sit beside him, and ordered the assembly to be seated. Naaharsingh asked one of his masked accomplices to sit next to him.

"Is there news of Birsingh?" Anirudhsingh asked.

"Yes, he was trapped with the King's traitorous men," Kharagsingh replied. "I got there and rescued him from their clutches. I have sent him to my camp. We should also get Bacchan Singh and Harihar Singh sent there under guard."

Kharagsingh's order was immediately carried out. The two dishonest men were handed over to a group of guards, and a brave chief led the party towards Kharagsingh's camp.

Kharagsingh then turned to Naaharsingh and questioned him. "So Karansingh's son is still alive? Can you produce him?"

"I have one proof of his being alive." Naaharsingh said.

"What is that?" Kharagsingh asked.

Naaharsingh took out a letter that had been tucked into his waistband. It was the letter he had confiscated from Ramdas, the man he had caught swimming. Kharagsingh's eyes reddened with anger as he read it.

"There is no question this is the King's hand," he said. "And it also has his seal. We do not need any more proof. It's all right even if I don't see Surajsingh in the flesh." He handed the letter to Anirudhsingh. "Read this, and pass it on."

After reading the letter, Anirudhsingh said, "Now we know, Sir, that the petition to the King of Nepal was not frivolous."

"It most certainly wasn't," Kharagsingh said. "By the way," he turned to Naaharsingh, "you said that people don't know the truth about Birsingh. What is that truth? Can you tell it now?"

"Yes I can," Naaharsingh said, "if I may have the attention of this council."

"Sure, we will hear you out," Kharagsingh said.

Naaharsingh told Kharagsingh and the chiefs the history of Karansingh and Karansingh Rathoo, and of his deliverance from death. He went on to tell them about his rescue of Birsingh, and then told them the story of Sundari that Tara had narrated to the sage. He had known quite a bit about Sundari; the rest he had learnt from Birsingh. In fact, Birsingh did not know that the Ahilya Tara had told him about was his own sister. It was Naaharsingh who had explained this to him.

Be that as it may, Naaharsingh's story left the men of the council disturbed and teary. Many of them swore at the dishonest Karansingh Rathoo. Their sorrow simmered for some time, and then they spoke together: "We will not serve this unjust King! We will punish him with our hands, and give the throne to the real Karansingh's son, Vijaysingh. We will collect funds and raise an army with Vijaysingh and Birsingh at its head!" They naturally called Naaharsingh by his original name.

Kharagsingh said that his army would also stand by Birsingh and Naaharsingh.

"There is a little more to tell you about my sister, Sundari," Naaharsingh said. "If you like, you can hear it. This gentleman"—he pointed to the man at his side—"is the one who brought it to my notice."

"Yes, of course we will hear you out," one of the chiefs said. "Who is this man?"

"He will tell you himself," Naaharsingh said.

"But he must unmask himself as well," Kharagsingh said.

"That is no problem," the man next to Naaharsingh said, as he removed his mask. He was none other than Babusahab, who had carried a boy to meet Sundari in the basement of the fort. The reader will not have forgotten him. He completed the story of Sundari.

"Under the name of Ahilya, Sundari stayed at this wicked King's palace for many days. The Queen got wind of the King's evil designs, and she sent Sundari to her father's place. She asked her father to get Sundari married, and he arranged her marriage to me. Sundari lived with me and we had a daughter and a son. The King did not find us for a long time, but he kept his men searching. Finally, they tracked her and kidnapped her. What they did with her, you have heard from Vijaysingh. It breaks my heart to think about how our poor daughter was killed. That King did many things to make Sundari let him have his way with her, but she did not betray her honour. Finally, the King locked her away in a secret room. He had a bowl full of our daughter's blood kept preserved with spices and placed right in front of her, so that she would see it and burn with remorse day and night. You can well imagine what that poor woman must have gone through, but that courageous Sundari—she did not stray from the path of virtue."

The council applauded Sundari's courage.

"When Sundari was imprisoned there, she had several girls watching over her. One of them took pity on Sundari. She risked her life to escape from there, reached me, and gave me Sundari's message. Sundari appealed to me to somehow take our son and meet her. As soon as I got the message, I came to this city and started working towards a clandestine visit. It took more than a year to organise this. I had to spend a lot of money to get men on my side. It has only been three or four days since I took my small boy, who was lucky to escape the wrath of the evil Karansingh, into that dungeon to meet Sundari. It was a coincidence that Naaharsingh chose the same day to rescue Birsingh. In fact, many of the guards knew about the rescue, but they were sympathetic to Birsingh and did not get in Naaharsingh's way.

"Sundari knew by then that Birsingh was her brother, but the King had her completely in his grasp. Sundari became even more worried when she heard of Birsingh's imprisonment. She was relieved to hear of his escape. I was talking to her in her cell when the King's flunky, that dishonest Harisingh, sauntered in. Sundari lost hope for her life and mine. I fought Harisingh and killed him. Then I wrapped his body in a blanket, and took help from one of the girls to carry my son. We were crossing a field when we met two of Naaharsingh's men. I was very keen to meet Naaharsingh and Birsingh, and Naaharsingh's men willingly took me with them. We buried Harisingh, the girl went back and I went on with the two men and my son to meet Naaharsingh. At that very moment, the King's men came upon the scene in hot pursuit of Naaharsingh, and we were lucky to be able to hide under a bridge and to survive to meet Naaharsingh and Birsingh."

"Where is the boy now?" Kharagsingh asked.

"He is the safe custody of Naaharsingh's men," Babusahab replied.

"I feel your pain," Kharagsingh said. "All of you are in very unfortunate situations. What I don't know yet is, where is Tara? What became of her?"

"I do know about Tara," Naaharsingh said, "but I haven't yet told Birsingh."

"Do you not consider it wise to talk about it still?" Kharagsingh asked.

"No, in fact I can talk about it," Naaharsingh said.

"Then please do," Kharagsingh said.

"From what you have heard, you will have followed that the King ordered Tara's father Sujan Singh to bring him Tara's head," Naaharsingh said.

"Yes, because Sujan Singh arrested the two girls but let Tara go," Kharagsingh said.

"True. But the King also wanted to let her live if she agreed to become his keep. Hari Singh was sent to convince Tara, but of course she did not agree. At the time when Sujan Singh was about to kill his own daughter in Birsingh's garden, I was there. A sage turned up at that very moment to help me save Tara. Tara is with him now."

"But why did you leave Tara with that sage?" Kharagsingh asked. "How do we know he can be trusted?"

"Oh, I have complete faith in him," Naaharsingh said. "He is a great soul. I confess I don't know where he is from, but he doesn't meet too many people, lives on his own in the jungle and is very fond of me. I have confided in him completely, and I often act with his advice. I also support him financially."

"Can I meet him?" Kharagsingh asked.

"I am not sure he will agree to that," Naaharsingh replied. He cast a look at the sky. "Morning is breaking. I cannot stay too long in the city."

"On the other hand, if you stay with me, it is no problem," Kharagsingh said.

"True, but there is no special benefit either. I will leave Birsingh in your protection, and take Babusahab with me. The two of us will return at the time and place you choose."

"That's fine," Kharagsingh said, "but there's one more thing."

"What's that?" Naaharsingh asked.

"When I was with the King, to rescue Birsingh, I thought it prudent to tell him that I would call a public hearing, a *durbar*, today and pronounce the death sentence on Birsingh and the other enemies of the state. I was, of course, leading him on, telling him what he wanted to hear. I told him that I would give him the title of *Adhiraja* on behalf of the King of Nepal. You know I had my reasons to say all this. What do you think?"

"You did well, Sir," Naaharsingh said. "This *durbar* will be fun. There will be a lot of action, and a bit of a riot. We will have to be prepared for battle. I suggest you postpone the *durbar* and be prepared. I will also use the time to strengthen my forces."

Kharagsingh looked at the councilmen. "What do you advise?"

"Naaharsingh is right," the chiefs said. "Let us use the day to reinforce ourselves. We should go into the *durbar* only when we are ready."

"Well, so it shall be," Kharagsingh said.

The men discussed a few more matters, and then dissolved the council. Naaharsingh took Babusahab with him, and the chiefs left for their homes. Kharagsingh reached his camp to find Birsingh conscious. He got his men to continue Birsingh's treatment while he apprised him of the events of the night.

# CHAPTER THIRTEEN

HEN KHARAGSINGH LEFT Karansingh's court after freeing Birsingh, one of the King's men, Saroopsingh, silently shadowed him till he met Naaharsingh.

Saroopsingh was startled, as he figured that Kharagsingh was playing a double game. He had told the King that he had arrested Naaharsingh, and here was Naaharsingh roaming free and talking to Kharagsingh. Saroopsingh saw that the two of them seemed friendly towards each other.

On the other hand, Saroopsingh was so scared at the very mention of Naaharsingh that he did not tarry for a moment. He ran back to the King and was panting by the time he reached the court.

"Well, what news?" Karansingh asked. "What makes you so breathless? Where have you been?"

"I followed Kharagsingh", Saroopsingh said.

"Why?"

"To see where he went, and to understand whether he is true."

"And what did you see?"

"He is completely dishonest. He has tricked you. He lied about arresting Naaharsingh. Naaharsingh is still a free man, and the two of them are friends. They met near the house where the council is being held. Naaharsingh had a few sturdy men with him, and they went in to the house, talking amiably."

"How did you know it was Naaharsingh?" Karansingh asked.

"Kharagsingh addressed him by name before they talked," Saroopsingh replied.

"Did Kharagsingh go there with Birsingh?"

"No, he sent Birsingh, escorted by his men, to his camp."

"So he completely fooled me!" Karansingh exclaimed.

"Without a doubt, Sir," Saroopsingh said.

"What a pity," Karansingh said. "He came here at a good time. If I had wanted to, I could have done away with him, and no one would have been the wiser for it." Saroopsingh said, "At this moment, Kharagsingh has taken Naaharsingh with him into the house where the council is in progress. If you give me a hundred men, I can arrest your enemies right away."

"Are you crazy?" Karansingh said. "The public will lose the little restraint that they have and there will be a revolt, which we won't be able to handle. Let us first get on firm ground. You went off to shadow Kharagsingh on your own without discussing it with me, but I also sent Shambhudutt after them. Let's see what news he brings. We can work out a solid plan once he returns. It's a pity I let myself be tricked."

The two of them continued to discuss strategies for a while. About half an hour after Saroopsingh's entry, Shambhudutt walked in. He looked harried and troubled.

"What news?" the King asked.

"The news is that a huge trick has been played. Kharagsingh has betrayed us. He got Birsingh sent to his camp and went straight to the house where your enemies are plotting against you. Naaharsingh met him on the way and accompanied him there."

"Well, this much we already know from Saroopsingh. What more do you have?" the King asked.

"How did Saroopsingh know?" Shambhudutt asked.

"Saroopsingh followed Kharagsingh. I did not know about it," the King said.

"But I do have another piece of news," Shambhudutt said.

"And what is that?"

"Bacchan Singh has been arrested, and Harihar Singh is also handcuffed."

The King was startled. "Is that so?"

"Yes, Sir," Shambhudutt said.

"And who had the temerity to do this?" the King asked.

"Who else but Kharagsingh?" Shambhudutt replied.

"Where are they now?" the King asked.

"They are in Kharagsingh's camp, under guard. I went close to the camp before returning."

"They've gone too far!" the King said. "Well, what does it matter. I will sort it out. I will not spare those scoundrels. And now I have the chance to openly accuse Kharagsingh. Summon the army chief. Tell him to be here on the double."

"Very well," Shambhudutt said.

"No wait, on second thought, that will take time," the King said. "I will go to him. You both follow me."

"Very well, Sir," Shambhudutt said.

The King stood up, ordered his clothes, and put on his weapons. The two men followed him as he walked out. The three men took horses, and rode towards the royal army cantonment. They rode like the wind, and soon they were at the army chief's bungalow.

The chief was intimated about the King's arrival. He came out looking flustered at the King's unprecedented and untimely visit, and stood before the King with palms joined. The King and his men dismounted and, after handing over the reins of their horses to the guards, walked in to the army chief's bungalow.

The men were in the bungalow for an hour. We do not know what kinds of arrangements they dwelled on. Well, we shall see what transpired as a result when the time comes. After an hour, the King stepped out, flanked by his men, and rode to the palace. The white of the morning had spread in the sky. The King had been up all night. His eyelids were heavy. He fell into a deep sleep as soon as he lay in bed, and he slept until a full watch after sunrise.

When Karansingh Rathoo opened his eyes, he felt a pang of sorrow. His heart was troubled and he could not spend a single moment without thinking of the events of the night. For a while, he was lost in thought as he sat there. With an effort, he stood up, finished the essentials and went into court after having bathed and eaten. He sent for his men and wrote a letter to Kharagsingh, in which he asked, "You spoke about a *durbar* and public hearing today. What time will it be held?" Saroopsingh was despatched to get a reply to this letter.

Kharagsingh was in his camp, conversing with some of the leading men of the city, when an orderly came in to announce the arrival of one of the King's men. Kharagsingh ordered him to be called in. When Saroopsingh came in and saw the assembly, he did his best not to show his dismay. He handed over the King's letter to Kharagsingh.

Kharagsingh wrote out an immediate reply: "In my opinion, a *durbar* today will not be feasible because the announcement has not yet been made in the city. I would like tomorrow to be announced as the day of the *durbar*, and today's time to be used to widely proclaim it. It will be appropriate to hold the hearing at night, and in your garden. Only the leaders of society may be called to the hearing."

When the King saw this letter, he asked Saroopsingh, "Well, by now we know Kharagsingh's every move is motivated. Tomorrow is a good day for me as well. But why at night, and why in the garden?"

"How do we know what lurks in his mind?" Saroopsingh said. "But I do know his motives are evil. I am sure he has a scheme."

"Whatever will happen, will happen," the King said. "Order the proclamation. We will also add *bahadur*, or brave, to our name. We certainly are not afraid. Our army will not fit into the garden, but it will be ready outside."

"He has called for a throne to be arranged. Perhaps to seat you after conferring the title upon you?"

"Yes, all that must be done, because we don't know what tricks he has up his sleeve. But this Karansingh is not unaware of those devils, nor is he such an innocent or coward who will let them walk over him!"

# CHAPTER FOURTEEN

NE WATCH OF THE NIGHT had passed. Kharagsingh sat in his camp, pondering over the plans for the hearing. Apart from about a score of local chiefs, Naaharsingh, Birsingh and Babusahab sat by his side.

"That's right," Kharagsingh said. "Even if our chiefs are outnumbered by the King's men, it does not matter."

"The King's heart will sink when I roar out my name," Naaharsingh said. "And besides, how much courage can a clearly guilty man, who has just been exposed, summon? He will lose half of his courage when he is reminded of his crimes publicly."

"We have also concluded that we will either free ourselves from that evil King, or die fighting," one of the chiefs said.

"God willing, that will not be necessary. Our task will be easy," Naaharsingh said. "Taking the King's life is no big matter. If I had wanted to, I could have sent him to hell by now. But I was waiting for today, for him to die after proving to the world that he is a bastard, and also showing them that evil begets evil."

Kharagsingh said, "By the way, you had said that the sage has agreed to meet me, and that he would be here by now. He hasn't turned up."

"He will, surely," Naaharsingh said.

At that very moment, a guard came in and said that a sage was waiting at the gate. Kharagsingh rose, and said, "We must show respect to such an altruist sage."

They all stood up and showed the sage in with deference. They seated him on the highest seat.

"You are troubling yourselves too much," the sage said. "I am just a wanderer, and I do not deserve this respect."

"You do not need to say that, Sir," Kharagsingh replied. "Naaharsingh has told us about you, and his words of praise found a place in my heart."

"Well, let's leave that aside," the sage said. "Tell me, you all had wanted to make arrangements for the *durbar*—are you ready now?"

"Yes, we are ready," Kharagsingh said. "The *durbar* will be tomorrow night at the King's big garden."

"I wish to attend it," the sage said.

"You are most welcome," Kharagsingh said. "Who can stop you?"

"But perhaps with these dreadlocks and moustache and my body caked in mud and ash... it may not be appropriate."

"It will be fine," Kharagsingh said.

"How does it matter if I give up my ascetic's looks for a day and look like a chief instead?" the sage asked.

"Who can have a problem with that?" Kharagsingh said with a laugh. "Kings and sages are considered equal anyway."

"No one else will have a problem, but Naaharsingh might," the sage said.

Naaharsingh immediately joined his palms in a *namaste*.

"I have no clue why you think so, Sir," he said.

"Well, Sir, you are the witness—Naaharsingh says he will not object," the sage said with a smile.

"I am very puzzled—why would he object?" Kharagsingh said.

"In that case, please summon a barber. We will see. But one more thing—can you and Naaharsingh please come with me to a quieter place and also get the barber there?"

Kharagsingh did as the sage wanted. The three of them went to one room, where the barber joined them. The sage got his hair cut, his beard shaved and his flowing moustache trimmed. Kharagsingh and Naaharsingh watched the spectacle.

*The sage got his hair cut, his beard shaved and his flowing moustache trimmed.*

As the sage's face started to peep through the thinning mask of hair, Naaharsingh's expression began to change. He struggled for words and then bowed, trembling, before the sage.

"Look!" the sage said. "I had said you would not stay quiet."

"No, I cannot be quiet," Naaharsingh said in a quavering voice. "I must speak!"

"Naaharsingh! What is this about?" Kharagsingh said.

"I told you so," the sage said. "Anyway, let the barber go. When there are only three of us, you can talk freely."

The barber went his way, and two servants were called to arrange a bath. The sage washed his hair, scrubbed himself well and donned the clothes Kharagsingh had arranged for him. During this time, Naaharsingh was visibly moved, but he kept his thoughts to himself. He controlled himself with a great effort, and waited for the sage to be ready to talk.

When the sage came out, the three men talked for an hour about things that we shall not reveal. But yes, we shall say that the sound of the three of them sobbing reached our ears and we still remember it like a dream.

When he emerged from the room and took leave, the sage had masked himself. Naaharsingh and Kharagsingh joined the rest of the group. The chiefs asked about the sage—where did he go? What was the outcome of his surprising request?

Kharagsingh said, "The sage has left for now. But he has said that he holds secrets in his gut that he will reveal in the *durbar*. So you will get to know them, together with me, tomorrow."

The men talked till midnight and then dispersed.

## Chapter Fifteen

LOT OF EFFORT had gone into the decoration of the royal garden. Bright lights turned the night into day. The path from the entrance of the garden to the fort was marked out by lights on both sides. Thousands of men thronged the garden. The city was abuzz with rumours. Some said that the King would get a title from the King of Nepal. Others said that it would be the day of reckoning for the King—the *durbar* would decide if the King was fit to rule. Many citizens wished that Birsingh would become King, and were even prepared to fight for him.

It seemed as if most of the city supported Birsingh, but the wise among them kept their opinions to themselves. Many leaders of the city had some inkling of what was to transpire at the *durbar*, but they kept mum as well.

The garden had a magnificent courtyard that was the planned venue for the *durbar*. The throne that Kharagsingh had requested was placed right in the middle of the courtyard. It was golden, and it had two silver chairs on either side. The chairs were for Karansingh and Kharagsingh. Facing the throne and these two chairs, there were two rows of silk-cushioned chairs for the city's aldermen. All the decorations worthy of the royal *durbar* were in place.

People started to trickle in as soon as the lamps were lit. By the time a watch of the night had passed, the *durbar* hall was full. Raja Karansingh and Kharagsingh took their seats. Naaharsingh, Birsingh and Babusahab were also in the *durbar*. The sage sat with a mask on. The men around him stared at him, and even Karansingh wondered who he was.

The King and his men did not recognise Naaharsingh, but Karansingh was furious to see Birsingh unchained. He bided his time, and he drew comfort from his two-thousand-strong army, which had surrounded the garden, and his men who were roaming the garden.

Kharagsingh's force of four hundred Nepalese men was also dispersed all around the garden, and Naaharsingh's hundred men had mingled in with the crowd. In the garden itself, there must have been two thousand men, out of which five hundred were the King's men. Once the *durbar* was filled to capacity, Kharagsingh rose and addressed the crowd in a loud voice.

"I, general of the King of Nepal, stand here to fulfil the duty for which I have been sent. Today's *durbar* has only two objectives. Firstly, minister Birsingh has been found guilty of the murder of the Prince and his sentence is to be pronounced. Secondly, King Karansingh is to be conferred the title of *Adhiraja*. You must be wondering why Birsingh, who has just been charged with a heinous crime, roams free without handcuffs and shackles. My reply to this is that he is firstly a minister of the Kingdom; secondly he cannot escape from this *durbar*. Thirdly, the King's men have wounded him so that he is weakened. Fourthly, Birsingh maintains that he will prove his innocence. Therefore, I order Birsingh to make his statement before the *durbar*." Kharagsingh took his seat, and Birsingh rose.

"You gentlemen know," Birsingh said, "and it is a popular saying, that a man who has lost hope of his life will speak from his heart, without fear. Today, I am in that situation. The King has falsely charged me with the murder of his son. In fact, he has hidden his son away. He is the one who has murdered his poor subjects, and he wants to frame me. You will ask why the King does so. The reply is that this King is the man who murdered my father. He was my father's servant, and he committed regicide to usurp my father's throne. At first this King was not scared of me, but when Naaharsingh started to harass him and the public gave me respect, Karansingh began to hatch a plot to kill me. It should also be known that Naaharsingh does not harass the King without good reason. He is my elder brother, and he seeks revenge for our father's murder." Birsingh went on to narrate the tale of Karansingh, Karansingh Rathoo, Naaharsingh, Sundari, Tara and related his own part in the story.

He continued: "Now you will want proof of these two facts—the false accusation against me, and the murder of my father. One of these will be provided by my elder brother Naaharsingh, whose real name is Vijaysingh. He is present in this *durbar*, and holds enmity against none except Karansingh Rathoo. The second will be proved by another man, who is probably somewhere here."

Birsingh's lengthy speech shocked the audience. Cries of "Shame!" filled the air. The King's heart sank. He was sure by now that the *durbar* had just one objective—to publicly expose him as a criminal. He guessed that the throne must also have especially been placed there to anoint Birsingh or Naaharsingh as King. He feared for his life, and wondered if fortune had chosen this moment to make him pay for his crimes.

"If I hadn't arranged for my army, it could definitely have gone badly for me. Well, I shall go down fighting," he thought. "But it's a good idea to wait. Let me see what they present as evidence. Which one of them is Naaharsingh? If he steps forward with the evidence, I will finally get to see him!"

*"Kill them all! Every one of them!" he shouted to his men.*

While the King pondered his options, Birsingh finished his speech. Naaharsingh, whom we shall now call Vijaysingh, stepped up immediately, gave the letter he had confiscated from Ramdas to Kharagsingh, and made the statement that he was submitting the first proof.

Kharagsingh stood up and read the letter aloud in a ringing voice. Then he raised the letter high, and he spoke: "We have clear evidence of one thing. This letter bears the King's sign and seal!" The audience was stunned for some time. "Shame on the King!" a voice rang out, and many others echoed this cry.

Kharagsingh had just sat down when the sage unmasked himself and strode to Karansingh's seat. He said loudly, "I am the second proof! This King only has to look at me to recognise me. But you all will be surprised to know that I am Karansingh, the father of Vijaysingh and Birsingh, the one whom Karansingh Rathoo had poisoned! My saviour's brother still lives in this city. If this King allowed it, I would tell you much more about my strange case, but I do not expect him to… Look, the scoundrel has leapt from his chair to attack me! The traitor is not ashamed, he—"

Why would the King let the sage finish? Karansingh Rathoo went berserk. With an unearthly shriek, he drew his sword and attacked the sage.

"Kill them all! Every one of them!" he shouted to his men. The sage dodged his assault, but the King's men charged at Birsingh and the others.

A pitched battle broke out and the floor turned bloody. Birsingh's men soon gained the upper hand.

Karansingh Rathoo had many men stationed in the garden, and his whole army outside, but they were not of much use to him. They did not have their hearts in the fight. The tales of the King's crimes had created dissent in the army, and the discussions of the *durbar* had disgusted them. Only a handful of them, who knew their lives were at stake, fought till the end. When Babusahab and Karansingh Rathoo came face-to-face, Babusahab threw Karansingh Rathoo to the ground and gouged out his eyes. Saroopsingh, Shambhudutt and Sujan Singh lost their lives. The fighting was intense but short-lived. The King's army did not get the chance to mobilise completely. Birsingh had despatched many enemy soldiers in spite of being wounded.

Kharagsingh led Birsingh to the throne and asked him to sit on it. He then loudly proclaimed, "At this moment, Birsingh, whom the people of Haripur love, has taken has taken the throne of Haripur. King Birsingh orders this fighting to stop, and all swords to be sheathed."

The fighting died down, and the people shouted their support for Birsingh. They jeered at the blinded Karansingh Rathoo.

# Chapter Sixteen

HE NEXT DAY, it became well known that the sage whose sight had frightened Karansingh Rathoo was none other than the real Karansingh, father of Birsingh and Vijaysingh. He revealed that when Karansingh Rathoo had got Sujan Singh to poison Karansingh, he had tried to win over all Karansingh's companions. A group of five men had pretended to defect to Karansingh Rathoo's side, but in their hearts they stayed loyal to Karansingh. When the poison knocked Karansingh out, Karansingh Rathoo had him buried and marched on. Karansingh was not dead yet.

After Karansingh Rathoo left, a Rajput named Dhanisingh, along with his servants, deliberately stayed behind. He dug up the grave and rescued Karansingh.

Karansingh lay in bed for five years before he recovered from the effect of the poison. For those five years, he lived in a different city and when he had recovered, he became a wanderer and an ascetic. However, he was never able to get Karansingh Rathoo off his mind. When Naaharsingh became famous, Karansingh shifted to the jungle near Haripur. He created circumstances that led to a meeting with Naaharsingh, but did not tell Naaharsingh his name.

Dhanisingh, Karansingh's saviour, had passed away, but his younger brother Anirudhsingh was a prominent citizen and readers will recall that this Anirudhsingh was active in the council meeting. Anirudhsingh was privy to many of Karansingh Rathoo's secrets, and he was a strong supporter of Birsingh, but he feared Karansingh Rathoo and he knew he had to bide his time before taking any decisive action.

That day was a day of great happiness. Karansingh was united with his two sons, his daughter, his son-in-law and his grandson, and he saw his younger son on the throne. Readers will ask here why Karansingh did not take the throne himself, and why the younger brother became King. We need to explain that when Karansingh, Kharagsingh and Vijaysingh conferred in secret, they discussed this topic. Karansingh had refused to rule, and Vijaysingh also refused Kingship, saying that he was not married and nor would he ever marry. Therefore, it was already decided that the throne would be given to Birsingh.

Those of Karansingh Rathoo's relatives who asked Birsingh for shelter were removed to a different building and their needs were arranged for. Sundari, who had been jailed in the basement, and Tara, who had been in the care of the real Karansingh, lived in the palace. Prince Surajsingh, Karansingh Rathoo's son, was never traced. No one knew where Karansingh Rathoo hid him away. Ramdas committed suicide, and Karansingh Rathoo only survived for a week after his encounter with Babusahab. Birsingh became a just and popular ruler.

# Afterword

## Devakinandan Khatri
## and the Making of the Hindi Novel

HE 1890S WERE IMPORTANT YEARS in the development of Hindi fiction. Devakinandan Khatri was creating a new class of readers with his fantasy thrillers. His contemporaries were etching their ideals for Hindu men and women in such moralizing works as *Devarani Jethani* ("Sisters-in-law"), *Nissahaya Hindu* ("The Helpless Hindu") and *Vama Shikshak* ("A Reader for Ladies"). Hindi crime fiction was also engendered in these years.

The diffusion of publishing houses went hand in hand with the growth of a new class of consumers who wanted to read in their leisure. The first A.H. Wheeler book stall opened in 1877 at the railway station in Allahabad, and by 1890 the chain had spread to practically every junction (a station that joined two different railway companies, and where passengers would spend a few hours waiting for connecting trains). To begin with, the stalls catered to the British passenger with the latest popular books, mostly detective and crime fiction. Gradually, educated Indians became customers, and started to demand the same genres in their mother tongues.

Books like *The Mysteries of London* found their way into translations and copies in Urdu and Hindi. It was Devakinandan Khatri who created a genre of mystery and fantasy grounded in Indian sensibilities. His books *Chandrakanta, Chandrakanta Santati* and *Bhootnath* blazed new trails in popularity. *Chandrakanta,* published in 1891, had had forty-five print runs by 1961[1]. These were times when the *nagari* script was struggling for existence. It had no official recognition; courts, schools and colleges were run in English and Urdu. Devakinandan Khatri did more than popularise Hindi fiction in these circumstances—he popularised Hindi. Many people learned Hindi just to read *Chandrakanta Santati*. Ramachandra Shukla, the first historian of

---

1. Gopal Rai (1965). *Hindi Katha Sahitya Aur Uske Vikaas Par Pathakon Ki Ruchi Kaa Prabhaav* ("Hindi Fiction and the Effect of Reader Preferences on its Development"), Patna: Granth Niketan.

Hindi fiction, writes, "In the beginning, his serialised fantasy novel became so famous that even those who did not read Hindi books became familiar with them... Devakinandan Khatri will be remembered in Hindi fiction as the man who created more readers than anyone else. No one knows how many Urdu speakers learned Hindi just to read *Chandrakanta Santati*."[2]

In fact, Devakinandan Khatri's Hindi was not the Hindi of pandits and their tomes. It was the "Hindustani" of the common people, cast into the *nagari* script. Mahatma Gandhi later adopted this language as a vehicle for the independence movement. Devakinandan Khatri himself wrote, "I cannot classify my Hindi, but I know that to read it, one does not need to reach out for a dictionary."[3]

Devakinandan Khatri was born in Muzaffarpur on 18 June. His ancestors were from Punjab, but had settled in Varanasi after Maharaja Ranjit Singh's death. Devakinandan Khatri's primary education was in Urdu and Farsi. He studied Hindi, Sanskrit and English later. Being from a wealthy business family, Devakinandan Khatri had the means to enjoy a life of travel, leisure and pursuits such as kite-flying. He was a contractor, and his work, which took him to the

---

2. Ram Chandra Shukla (1940). *Hindi Sahitya Ka Itihaas* ("The History of Hindi Fiction"), Allahabad: Indian Press.

3. In his introduction to *Chandrakanta Santati*.

jungles of Chakiya and Naugarh, was not only a source of income—it also exposed him to the dense, hilly forests and historic ruins of the region. His bond with the atmosphere of those parts became a source of inspiration for the fantasy elements in his work later.

He wrote the first part of *Chandrakanta* in 1888. Encouraged by the response, he completed the story in four parts. He moved on to the stories of Chandrakanta and Virendra Singh's children, *Chandrakanta Santati*, told in twenty-four parts and serialised from 1894 to 1905 in his magazine *Upanyas Lahari* ("Novel Currents"). He also planned to use *Bhootnath*, a character from *Chandrakanta* as the basis for another series of novels. His death in August 1913 interrupted this series when he had only written six instalments. His son Durgaprasad Khatri completed *Bhootnath* after his death.

Apart from the landmark works *Chandrakanta, Chandrakanta Santati* and *Bhootnath,* Devakinandan Khatri wrote *Narendra-Mohini, Kusum Kumari, Birendraveer* or *Katora Bhar Khoon* ("The Bowl Full of Blood"), *Kajar Ki Kothri* ("The House of Kohl") and *Gupt Godna* ("The Hidden Tattoo"). Lahari Press, the publishing house he opened in 1898, and which published *Upanyas Lahari,* and the serialization of *Chandrakanta Santati* and *Bhootnath,* is still active.

Devakinandan Khatri's unparalleled popularity was founded on the characteristics of his novels. Many of his works rely on the constructs of the *tilasm* (magical maze) and the *aiyyar* (spy-magician).[4] *Chandrakanta, Chandrakanta Santati* and *Bhootnath* have plots built around the loves of princes and princesses, and the webs of intrigue and treasure hunts that surround these lovers. These novels contain long chains of mysterious, fantastical and thrilling episodes. The protagonists infiltrate each other's camps in disguise, untangle complicated situations and win huge treasures, while vanishing every now and then. It is likely that Devakinandan Khatri was influenced by works such as the ancient *Daastaan-e-Amir-Hamza* and the nineteenth century *Tilasm-e-Hoshrubaz* that were popular in Urdu.

However, the consensus among critics is that Devakinandan Khatri's style and objectives are not just different from these earlier works; they are poles apart. Devakinandan Khatri's objectives were not religious—they were most worldly. Knowing that his readers were less likely to believe in the supernatural than those of the earlier *Mir-Hamza*, he took pains to establish the bases for the events that seemed supernatural or superhuman. He sought to allay the doubts of readers with a scientific temper, and to portray fantasy liberated from the constraints of superstition and sorcery. He created a modern, printing-enabled rendition of the Urdu *daastaan*

-------

4. Devakinandan Khatri defined these constructs in his introduction to *Chandrakanta.*

(chronicle) tradition. It was only natural that the listener addressed in the *daastaan* would be replaced by the reader in Devakinandan Khatri's work.

Some critics see Devakinandan Khatri's novels as more than entertainments. Rajendra Yadav, for example suggests that they were a feeble attempt to demonstrate Indian intellectual strength after the crushing defeat of the revolt of 1857.[5]

In complete contrast to the *tilasmi-aiyyari* works (*Chandrakanta, Chandrakanta Santati* and *Bhootnath*), *The Bowl Full of Blood,* written in 1895, tells the story of the decline and fall of the unjust and cruel King Karansingh. This King turns out to be an impostor whose nefarious plans fail as the forces of good prevail over those of evil. The rightful King's family, which was torn apart by the fake Karansingh's machinations, is reunited and the honest, brave and popular Birsingh takes the throne. The novel's setting is the Tarai region of Bihar and Nepal.

Devakinandan Khatri spins the sixteen-chapter story in a very interesting way—the unravelling of the awful truth about the fake Karansingh is completed as the past is narrated from different points of view, and the forces of good answer the call of duty by taking up arms against their evil oppressor. A council is formed to end the evil

---

5. Rajendra Yadav (1981), *Atharah Upanyaas* ("Eighteen Novels"), Delhi: Akshar Prakashan.

King's reign. This device signals Devakinandan Khatri's modern view that the people have the right to dethrone an unfit King. The council can also be viewed as a democratic entity, and one that had a special significance in British Raj era.

The good versus evil conflict in *The Bowl Full of Blood* is reflected in a black and white view of the world, with no room for shades of grey. The "white" aspects of the story occur during the day, while the black aspects naturally happen in the night. Consider for example, this passage from Chapter 1:

> "It was past midnight, and dark clouds had laid an inky shroud on the earth. In the deathly quiet, the only sound was that of the rustling of leaves as the gusts of wind shook them. A man hidden inside a cluster of grape vines mumbled the above words to himself. What did he look like? It is difficult to say right now, dear reader. Firstly, the dark night hid him well. Secondly, he was swathed in black clothes. Thirdly, the leaves of the grape vines formed a curtain that hid his features."

Good and evil, black and white: it seems that in Devakinandan Khatri's mind the dividing line was firm and uncompromising, and he deftly used light and darkness to buttress this theme of conflict. This translation takes you on a journey to a period when the diffusion of Hindi crossed a tipping point with the mass adoption of a new habit—the reading of Hindi. I hope you enjoyed the journey.

Balwant Kaur, Ph.D.
Assistant Professor
Miranda House, Delhi University
New Delhi, India

# Glossary

| | |
|---|---|
| Adhiraja | King of kings |
| Brahman | Priestly caste |
| Dhoti | Long loincloth tied at the waist |
| Durbar | Royal council with courtiers in attendance |
| Namaste | Sign of greeting in which one joins the palms in front of the chest, with the fingers pointing upwards |
| Neem | Tree of the Mahogany family, native of the Indian Sub continent |
| Indra | God of rain and thunder |
| Raja | King |
| Tilak | A mark worn on the forehead |
| Watch | Unit of time, approximately three hours |